MOON KISSED

Mirror Lake Wolves - Book One

JENNIFER SNYDER

MOON KISSED
MIRROR LAKE WOLVES – BOOK ONE

© 2017 by Jennifer Snyder
Editing by H. Danielle Crabtree
© 2017 Cover Art by Cora Graphics
© Shutterstock.com/ Svyatoslava Vladzimirska

Author Note:
This is a work of fiction. The characters and events in this book are fictitious.
Any similarity to real persons, living or dead, is coincidental and not intended
by the author. The author acknowledges the trademarked status and
trademark owners of various products referenced in this work of fiction,
which have been used without permission. The publication/use of these
trademarks is not authorized, associated with, or sponsored by the trademark
owners.

ISBN-13: 978-1974155071
ISBN-10: 1974155072

1

The flickering letters in the sign hung above Eddie's bar pulsed with my heartbeat. Somehow, the strobing neon lights had become one of the things I could always count on never changing. There was another thing I could count on when it came to Eddie's too—Dad being shit-faced somewhere inside.

It was a given on any day that ended in the letter Y.

I leaned back in my seat and willed my heart to stop hammering against my rib cage. As much as I didn't want to step inside, I knew I had to. There was no one else. Everyone was sick of my father's antics, and to be honest, I couldn't blame them. While I was sick of his shit too, I was still his daughter. We were family. It was the only reason I was here. The only reason I ever came.

I shouldn't be here, though.

I wasn't of legal age to drink. I was barely eighteen, but no one in Eddie's would care. All they wanted was the town drunk to leave the bar so they could resume their night of fun without listening to him blabber about the past.

There was another reason I shouldn't be here besides not being of legal drinking age—Alec. I should be enjoying my night with him. We were supposed to see a movie and spend time together. Yet here I was, picking up my dad from the bar for the third night this week. When would Eddie learn to cut Dad off? Why did he always let him get so shit-faced?

The door to the bar swung open, garnering my attention and revealing a lone figure in the threshold. The guy's face was shrouded in shadows, but it didn't matter. I didn't need to see it to know who he was.

I'd recognize Eli Vargas anywhere.

Something about him called to me in a way I didn't understand. A way that made me uneasy. I'd tried over the years to place distance between us, but it never seemed to matter. One way or another, we were always pulled into the same space despite how hard I tried to stay away from him.

Eli sauntered toward my car. A shiver, one that was hard to pinpoint why it occurred, slipped along my spine as I watched him draw nearer. It was always that way with Eli. My body betrayed me when he was around. Something about him spoke to a darker place inside me, a feral place. A primal place entirely free of inhibitions and responsibilities. I constantly pushed away those feelings so I could feel a sense of normalcy.

As Eli grew closer, the lamppost a few feet from where I'd parked illuminated him. My insides vibrated to life as I drank him in. Dressed in low-hung jeans and a gray tank top that showcased his beautiful muscles glistening in the moonlight,

Eli was mouthwatering. Even so, my brain itched for me to place distance between us. Maybe it was because of the way my body reacted when I was in his presence—electrically charged and utterly out of my control. He'd always represented trouble to me. Any guy who looked good enough to elicit such a feeling from me by simply being in his presence couldn't be anything besides trouble. He was the type of guy who left a string of broken hearts behind once he got what he wanted.

At least, that's how I viewed him. Maybe I was wrong, but I wasn't about to risk it. Not with him. Not with the way I always seemed to feel while in his presence.

Eli leaned against my car door and folded his arms across his chest. My window was down, and I waited for him to say something. His voice slipping through the night would cause a reaction inside me no voice ever should. My fingers gripped the steering wheel until my knuckles turned white. He remained mute, but his eyes were fixed on me. I could feel them. The heat of them. The pull they harbored.

It had my adrenaline spiking and stole the breath from my lips.

A loud crash came from somewhere inside the bar, causing me to flinch. It snapped me out of my head and forced me back to reality. I hoped Dad hadn't broken something again. If so, I wasn't sure how we would pay for it this time.

Shouting and low grumbles made their way through the thin walls of the place. It sounded as though my father was well beyond inebriated and had overstayed his welcome with the other patrons.

How much had they allowed him to drink tonight? Was it

Eli's fault? After all, he was the newly hired bartender. Which also meant I'd be seeing a lot more of him.

The stupid universe pulling us together again.

Another round of ruckus burst from inside the place. I needed to get Dad home before he got himself into trouble. While it was true my dad had issues, I was blaming tonight's excessive alcohol consumption on Eli. He knew my dad enjoyed drinking like a fish. He shouldn't have served him as much as he obviously had.

My gaze drifted to Eli, ready to tell him that. A smirk, which caused my lower stomach to heat, twisted across his beautiful face, and my mouth went dry. Thoughts vanished as though they'd never existed.

I pulled myself together. It was something I'd learned to do at the drop of a hat while in his presence. Why was he grinning like that? Was he glad I was here? Suspicion built inside me. Had he allowed my dad to get beyond shitty on purpose? He did know I had plans with Alec tonight. I knew he'd overheard us the other night when Alec was dropping me off. Eli had been sitting outside his parents' trailer. I wondered if this was his way of sabotaging my date tonight. Even though Eli and I had never been an item, it still seemed like something he would do. He didn't like Alec. In fact, he'd told me more than once he thought I was wasting my time with him.

A tiny part of me thought he might be right, considering Alec was human, but I'd never admit it.

I popped open my car door and forced myself out. Eli took a step back, giving the door room to swing wide, but the smirk never left his face. The bright green of his eyes captured my attention, pulling me in like always. Eli had an

4

otherworldly eye color I had never witnessed on anyone. There was something mysterious and beautiful about it.

"Mina Ryan," he muttered in a sultry, low voice that caused goose bumps to erupt across my skin. "Look at you, all dressed up like you have somewhere to be."

Butterflies burst to life in the pit of my stomach, but I forced myself to ignore them. To ignore the effect Eli Vargas had on me entirely.

I was dressed up, but it wasn't for him. It was for Alec. He knew it, too. The cocky glint shimmering in his hypnotic eyes let me know.

"Yeah, yeah," I said as I slipped past him toward the bar. The scent of stale cigarettes lingered in the night air the closer to the door I came. The place was supposed to be non-smoking indoors, like every public place in town, but no one ever obeyed that law. There was even a sign posted behind the bar, but it didn't matter. People smoked when they drank in Eddie's; it was a fact. "Just tell me where my dad is."

"Feeling a little feisty this evening, I see." He followed me toward the bar closer than he should. I swore I could feel his hot breath tickle the fine hairs along the back of my neck. It made me want to rip my ponytail out to block the sensation; it had my knees going weak.

I glanced over my shoulder at him. "Wonder why."

Eli's gaze dipped to the gravel of the parking lot. Did he feel bad now? "He's at the end of the bar."

"Thanks." I swung open the screen door and stepped inside.

My eyes scanned the smoke-filled, dimly lit place as I walked farther in. A variety of sympathetic and pissed-off looks were tossed my way. I knew it was because some felt bad for my dad while others felt bad for me. There were also those who wished I would have come earlier so they could enjoy their night escaping their demons without my dad interrupting.

Deep down, though, they all knew that was also the reason my dad was here. He was escaping his demons. Didn't that make everyone here doing the same a damn hypocrite?

Dad used to be one of Mirror Lake's best mechanics, but a freak accident when I was twelve nearly cost him his life. Instead, it had left him crippled. The doctors had said he would never walk again. He'd be paralyzed from the waist down for the rest of his life, but what they didn't know was my dad wasn't an average man. He wasn't your average human, either.

Neither was I.

The Ryans came from a long line of something special. At least that was how Gran always described it. I'd always thought of it as something different, not special. In a place like Mirror Lake, being different isn't exactly uncommon. I guess I should be thankful.

That something special healed my dad better and faster than the doctors thought possible. He became a medical mystery in their eyes. A miracle. His spinal injury healed in a couple of months, not entirely, but enough for him to walk again, albeit with a limp. At least he wasn't wheelchair-bound like they'd thought he would be. The something special in our blood hadn't healed his pain, though. That's what crip- pled him most. He quickly became addicted to the pain medications they had him on, eating them like candy while trying to dull his pain to a bearable level.

It never lasted long.

He'd eat a handful and then complain an hour later he was still hurting. The doctors couldn't understand why his body metabolized the medication so quickly, but we all knew. The something special in our blood could be seen as a curse in my dad's case. It was because of it nothing lasted in his system as long as it should. Gran said there were alternative medicines he could take to alleviate his pain besides the death pills the doctors prescribed him, but he refused to try anything else.

Instead, he turned to alcohol.

He'd told me once, when I'd asked why he drank so much, if he drank enough he couldn't hardly feel anything.

I'd cried for him that night.

It had been six years since the accident. Six years since he'd let the alcohol and pills take over his life. Six years I'd watched both do more harm than good.

My lips pursed together when I spotted him sitting at the end of the bar.

"Bout time you came back, Eli," Dad slurred. His blood-shot eyes bypassed me and landed on Eli. "Need a refill."

"No. You're done. Let's get you home," I said as I stepped to his side.

"Mina, my little Mina Bena," he slurred, finally having noticed me. His face erupted into a large smile as I draped his arm over my shoulders. "You look so pretty tonight. Doesn't she look pretty, Eli?"

My cheeks heated. I refused to make eye contact with Eli. I didn't want to see the smirk I knew would be plastered on his face.

"All right, Dad. Come on," I said as I tried to force him to stand. This was going to be harder than usual. He'd had way too much to drink tonight. His limbs were practically made of rubber.

"That she does, Mr. Ryan," Eli surprised me by saying; I hadn't expected him to answer. Especially not with something that sounded so genuine.

My gaze flicked toward him. I'd only meant to glance at him for a split-second, but his eyes were trained on me from the other side of the bar. The same genuine sensation I gathered from the tone of his voice had somehow found its way to his eyes. It swirled within their depths. The sight of them startled me. I held his gaze longer than I should. My grip on my dad loosened, and he fell to the floor.

"Oh my God, I'm so sorry! Are you okay, Dad?" I bent to help him up at the same time I noticed Eli jump the bar. His fingertips grazed mine as he reached to help my dad to his feet, causing that same strange electricity to fizzle across my skin that always seemed to happen each time we touched. I jerked my hand back, releasing the hold I had on my dad for the second time. This time his head hit the leg of the barstool he'd been sitting on. Dad erupted in a fit of laughter as my face became impossibly hot.

What was wrong with me tonight?

"Here, let me help." Eli grabbed my father by the shoulders and lifted him to his feet. He was strong, there was no doubt, but I wasn't a damsel in distress. I could take care of my dad. Hell, I had been for the last few years.

All I needed was for Eli to keep his distance. It was when he was too close, and paying more attention to me than he should, issues spurred.

"I don't need any help. I've got it," I muttered as soon as

Eli had my dad standing again. "Thanks for calling me. Next time try not to serve him so much alcohol."

"Not a problem, and I'm pretty sure he'd already been drinking when he came in." Eli grabbed my dad's cane and handed it to me. I could barely release my grip on him long enough to grab hold of it and tuck it beneath my arm. While my dad wasn't overweight, he was a big guy. At six foot, he towered over me. Granted, I was all of five-foot-two, but he also had at least a hundred pounds on me.

Regardless, I'd helped him out of this bar more times than I cared to remember.

The first time he'd called me from the bar asking if I would pick him up, I'd been fourteen. Scared shitless didn't even describe how I felt sitting behind the wheel when I drove over, but I liked the feeling of someone counting on me. Someone needing me. Especially family.

Maybe that was my issue, my own inner demon. I cared more than I should about those I loved.

"How did he get here?" I knew he hadn't driven. His truck was still at home. I couldn't imagine him walking the distance either. It was a good six or seven miles. Then again, I wouldn't put it past him to try. He was nothing but determined when he had his mind set on something.

"He came in with Herschel Ammons a couple hours ago. Both of them looked like they were drunk as a skunk. Herschel tried to leave, but I took his keys from him and called Betty Sue. She got him about thirty minutes before you got here. If I'd known you were going out on a date or whatever, I would've had her take your dad home, too."

I had Dad start walking toward the exit, leaning on me as

we went. It felt like every bone in my right shoulder was being crushed by his deadweight, but I refused to let Eli help.

"Cut the crap. You knew I was going out tonight," I snapped, flashing him the best go-to-hell look I could muster while carrying my dad's weight.

"What if I did?" A devious grin spread across his face. "What are you going to do about it?"

"Nothing. I'm sure if I did, you'd like it too much."

"No truer words have ever been spoken," he said with a wink.

I pushed the screen door to the bar open and eased my way out with Dad still in tow. He had practically passed out on me and was of no assistance whatsoever. He muttered something about my mom, and I knew that was why he'd drank so much tonight. He'd been thinking about her again. No doubt blaming himself for why she'd left us.

The thought of her boiled my blood, giving me the added oomph I needed to get him to my car.

"Can you at least let me open your door for you?" Eli asked from somewhere behind me. I hadn't realized he'd followed me out.

"No, I've got it. Go back to work," I insisted. I leaned my dad against my old hatchback as best I could. My fingers wrapped around the door handle, and I lifted up before I pushed the button, knowing it was the only way to get the passenger door open. "You wouldn't have been able to figure out how to open it anyway."

"Thanks for the vote of confidence, but I've seen you do that a time or two in the past. Think I could've managed."

"What, are you stalking me now?"

"Stalking you, no. Have you forgotten I've lived in the trailer beside your Gran's my entire life?"

Of course I hadn't forgotten. How could I ever forget someone like him living beside me my entire life? "Right."

I pulled the passenger door open all the way. It protested with a loud squeak, but thankfully managed to stay open on its own. "Come on, Dad. Let's get you home," I said as I grabbed him by the shoulders, hoping to steer him through my passenger door with ease.

"So pretty. Just like your mother," Dad murmured. "You've got her eyes."

"Yeah, thanks, Dad. I know," I said as I gave him a final shove. He fell into the seat, pulling me along with him. The car shook, causing the door to start to close. I squeezed my eyes shut, preparing for the painful blow of the metal door against my calf, but it never came.

Eli had stopped it from crushing my leg. "Here, please let me help." His hands gripped my waist as he helped me to my feet. Electricity sizzled along my skin, causing my heart rate to spike.

I fumbled out of the way and allowed him to maneuver my dad around in the seat the right way. A gentle breeze blew, wafting Eli's masculine scent to me. My eyes followed his every movement as my stomach fluttered. Jesus, what was it about this guy that invoked all these crazed sensations inside me?

Alec. I needed to think of Alec.

Eli's help meant nothing besides me getting to see Alec sooner. I'd already had to cancel movie plans with him. I didn't want to have to cancel the entire night, and if I didn't get help situating my dad in my passenger seat, that was what

I'd have to do. My time was running short. I couldn't stand him up again. I'd already rearranged our plans twice this week. He didn't seem to mind, but I knew having to do it a third time might bother him. He would probably think I was a flake and quit giving me the time of day.

I didn't want that. I liked Alec too much to allow it to happen.

He was a good guy. He made me feel peaceful and content. Normal in some unexplainable way I always seemed to crave. He made me feel more than what I was.

And, he was the exact opposite of Eli Vargas.

Where Eli was dark and mysterious, Alec was sweet and charming. Where Eli was cocky and primal, Alec was southern and respectful.

They were like night and day.

"There, got him in for you, but I didn't buckle him up. Figure that's something you can do yourself," Eli said as he eased away from my car and closed the door.

"Thanks." As much as I hated to admit it, I was glad he'd helped. It was clear I'd needed someone. My dad was hammered. Again.

Gran would be pissed. Her anger wouldn't last though; it never did. She felt as bad for him as the rest of us. Probably more. After all, he was her son.

"You do look nice tonight, Mina," Eli said as I started around the front of my car. His words gave me pause. What was with all his compliments lately? While he had always tossed them at me from time to time, there'd never been so many strung together, and they'd never made me feel the way they did tonight—all hot and bothered. "I'm sorry if I held you up long enough to ruin your plans with that boy. I honestly didn't mean to. I thought to ask Betty Sue to take your dad home two seconds too late." He rubbed the back of his neck as his eyes lifted from the gravel to lock on mine. The light of the waxing crescent moon above illuminated his face more than the lamppost, making it easy to see how genuine his words were in case I couldn't hear it in his voice.

"You didn't ruin my night. *That boy* will wait for me," I said, tossing the words he'd used when speaking of Alec back in his face. He knew his name. Why was it so hard for him to say it?

"If he knows what's good for him, he better." Eli grinned.

I didn't know if he meant he'd beat him up if he didn't or something else altogether. I didn't wait around to find out either. Instead, I rounded my car and slipped behind the wheel. My fingers fumbled with the keys, but only because my eyes had drifted back to Eli. He was watching me, working his jaw like there might be more he wanted to say. I didn't give him the chance. I cranked the engine of my car. It whined before sputtering to life. My dad stirred in the passenger seat and laughed as he mimicked the noise my clunker made. I wished he'd sober up long enough to fix the damn thing for me.

I wasn't about to hold my breath for it, though.

Gears ground together as I shifted into reverse. I backed out of my parking spot without another glance at Eli and shifted into drive, ready to head home.

The second I passed the sign for Mirror Lake Trailer Park, I checked the dashboard clock. Alec hadn't sent me a text yet, but I was sure he would soon. I was creeping up on being well beyond fashionably late and bordering on rude.

Another date had been ruined, and it was my fault.

I cut the engine on my hatchback and hurried to the passenger side so I could get my dad out. Somewhere along the stretch between Eddie's and home, he'd fallen asleep. His head fell back, letting his mouth hang open, and he sawed logs as drool dribbled from his mouth. This was nothing new. He'd always snored, but when he drank, it was worse.

"Dad, wake up. We're home," I muttered as I nudged him. He didn't budge. "Dad! Wake up!" I said louder. He folded his arms over his chest and proceeded to roll over onto his side.

My patience was wearing thin. I needed him to wake up so he could help me get him inside. There was no way I'd be able to carry him the way Eli had.

"Dad! Get up!" I shouted as I gave him a shove. I didn't care if I woke up the neighbors three feet away in the next trailer. It was just Eli's family, and they were probably used to it by now.

"Hmmm?" Dad stirred, but he didn't fully commit to staying awake.

It took one more hard shove before he finally came to enough to help maneuver himself out of my car. His balance was off. I blamed it equally on his bum leg and how much he'd drank, but knew it had more to do with the latter.

When I finally got him inside the quiet recesses of our trailer, I flopped him down on the couch. There was no point in trying to take him back to his room. It would only wake up Gran. Thank goodness the room my little sister and I shared was on the other side of the trailer. The last thing I wanted was for her to see Dad this wasted. It would only upset her. It was hard enough being thirteen and not having your mom around—I remembered from personal experience—but it was another thing altogether to be constantly reminded of how screwed up your dad was because your mom was gone. Plus, I didn't think seeing her older sister drag her drunk dad into the house was a memory I wanted her to have.

I tried to spare her as much as I could.

Maybe it was wrong to shelter Gracie as much as I did, but I didn't want her to hurt. I couldn't stand seeing those I loved hurt. Most of all, I didn't want Gracie to worry. I knew she wasn't stupid. She saw what went on around here, but keeping as much from her as possible made me feel like I was doing something good. Like I was making things better for her. It had to count for something, right?

I placed my hands on my hips and blew a few strands of brown hair that had slipped from my ponytail out of my eyes. Carrying Dad in had been tough. I was definitely going to be sore tomorrow. My fingertips reached around to knead the already tender muscles of the shoulder I thought Dad had broken. My cell vibrated in my back pocket, and I knew it had to be Alec. He was probably texting to say we'd have to reschedule. Either that or he was wondering where the hell I was. I wanted to explain everything to him, but I didn't know how. Telling the guy you liked you came from a screwed-up family, one where you had to rescue your dad from himself nearly every night, was not a topic I cared to discuss.

It wasn't normal.

And that was all Alec was—normal. It had drawn me to him. How completely normal everything about him and his life seemed. He had a good home life and loads of friends. Everything I craved to surround myself with because my life was lacking in the normal department greatly. Even if you stripped away my home life dynamics, there still wasn't a shred of normalcy to be found. Not with my family's secret. Heck, not with everyone in the trailer park's secret.

I reached for my cell. Alec's name lit my screen and so did his text.

Hey, I was wondering if you still wanted to do something tonight. It's getting a little late.

I glanced at the time. Yeah, it was getting late. Damn it. It had taken me too long to get my dad. Anger bubbled inside me. Dad mumbled something about my mom in his sleep and shifted around to cuddle one of the throw pillows. All my anger dissipated.

He was hurting. Not just physically, but mentally.

The sad fact was he'd probably never get over either ailment. Not the pain from the accident that still lingered or the pain from my mom leaving.

I didn't blame him. Instead, I blamed her.

If she were still here, things might not be as bad. How could a woman abandon her kids the way she did? How could she walk away from her family? Her husband?

I understood sometimes parents don't stay together, that sometimes it didn't work out the way they wanted, but it didn't work that way with kids. You don't get to divorce them. You don't get to leave. Once you're a parent, you're always a parent.

Yeah, I still want to do something. – Mina

I hit send and waited for Alec to respond, hoping he didn't ask what I wanted to do. Deciding on plans had never been my forte. My immediate response was always, "I don't know." It drove Gran mad.

Cool, want to meet at Rosemary's?

Rosemary's was a mom-and-pop diner in town. Everyone went there to hang out. Everyone except me. I didn't have issues with the people who hung out there. The place just wasn't my cup of tea. Being in a brightly lit, crowded place was never something I enjoyed. I preferred quiet places in nature, dim lighting, and small crowds.

Alec was the exact opposite. Maybe that was another reason I liked him. He forced me out of my comfort zone. He was a people person. The perfect mixture of outgoing and sweet.

Sure, meet you there in twenty. – Mina

"Mina, honey? Is that you?" Gran's voice floated to my ears from down the hall. She appeared in the kitchen dressed in her baby blue bathrobe and fuzzy white slippers. Her gray hair cascaded past her shoulders in soft curls and her face was wrinkled with age, but it was the concern tinting her blue eyes a shade lighter than usual that hurt my heart. She was going to be upset when she saw my dad laid out on the couch, but what could I do? There was no way to shield her from it. If she heard me come in, then she already knew the reason why. "You had to go get him again, didn't you?" she asked, her tone sharp.

"Yeah."

"He's getting worse."

"I know." Sometimes I wondered if I'd wake up to find he'd died of a broken heart.

"Thank you for bringing him home again, dear, but you could have woken me up. I would've gone for him," she said, giving me the stern look I considered her signature stare in situations like this.

"I don't mind."

"Still, I don't feel it's your place. I've told you that before."

She had. A thousand times. Same as all the other times before, I ignored her. There was no way I'd send my seventy-year-old grandmother to a bar in the middle of the night to pick up her drunk son. It didn't seem right.

"You look nice. Are you going out tonight?"

"Yeah. I was supposed to meet Alec hours ago for a movie, but that obviously didn't happen. Now I guess we're meeting at Rosemary's."

Gran's wrinkled lips pinched into a frown. "I don't know why you waste your time with that boy."

And here we go. Just like Eli, Gran called Alec that boy. I was so sick of hearing those words. I didn't know why everyone insisted on me blowing him off. Alec was a decent guy. He made me happy. Shouldn't that be all that mattered?

"I like him. Isn't that enough?" I asked, minding my tone. Gran would get onto me if I didn't. Then there was no way I'd be permitted to leave the house, eighteen or not. Gran ruled the roost.

"You know it's not, Mina. Nothing good can come from spending so much time with him. Especially not with the next full moon coming so soon." She stepped to a cabinet in the kitchen and pulled down a mug. Every muscle in my body tensed at the reminder of the coming moon. "I love you, child, but you're only setting yourself up for heartbreak." She filled the mug with tap water before placing it in the microwave, and then moved to another cabinet to retrieve her favorite homemade tea blend. "You know there's a strong chance you're Moon Kissed. It runs in our family's blood."

"I know," I whispered as icy panic set in at the thought of another full moon passing and nothing happening.

I wanted to be Moon Kissed, but I also wanted the normal life Alec represented. Shouldn't I be able to have both?

2

I pulled into the parking lot of Rosemary's later than I would have liked. Somehow, I'd hit every red light between the diner and my place. I hoped Alec was still here. I scanned the lot, searching for a parking spot and noticed his red truck near the back. Relief flooded my system.

A warm breeze kicked up as I slipped out of my car. It ruffled the fine hairs framing my face as I made my way to the double doors of Rosemary's. Charbroiled burgers and grease hung heavily in the air. My stomach growled as I continued to walk, reminding me I'd forgotten to eat dinner.

Laughter and meaningless chatter drummed from inside the building as a group of guys I recognized from school made their way out the door. The short one in the middle smiled at me as his eyes appraised my body. While I wasn't as self-conscious as most girls, it did make me wonder if I'd tried too hard tonight when deciding on an outfit. My skinny jeans were tight, but not painted on. However, I didn't think my jeans had garnered his attention. I was sure it was the turquoise tank top, which dipped low in the front revealing my cleavage, that had him staring.

Maybe it would work in my favor and make Alec forget how much I'd screwed up our night.

The moment I stepped inside, my senses were assaulted. Burgers sizzled on the grill, people chatted too loudly from booths and tables, silverware clinked against plates and bowls as people ate, and a couple at a booth just inside the doors argued. I pulled in a deep breath and glanced around for Alec. It didn't take me long to spot him. He was at the counter, chatting with the girl working behind it. I recognized her face, but I couldn't think of her name. Tiny pinpricks of jealousy slipped through me at the sight of them together. Whatever she'd said made him laugh, and my jealousy bloomed as his head tipped back, revealing his pearly whites.

God, he was beautiful.

His light brown hair glistened in the fluorescent lights, and his tanned skin looked kissable. He wore a pair of blue jeans like always, a plain T-shirt, and a pair of scuffed-up hunting boots.

I stepped closer, watching and waiting to see if he'd feel my presence or maybe my eyes on him. Everyone else always seemed to. I chalked it up to having something to do with the special genes that floated through my DNA. Sometimes it made people leery of the others and me.

Alec noticed me when I was about three feet away from him, but only because the girl he'd been talking to had noticed me first. He was curious to see what had garnered her attention so suddenly. She was observant; I'd give her that. I searched my mind again for her name, but couldn't remember it still. I'd seen her with Alec before. She'd been chummy with him then too. Maybe I'd seen them together at school. There was a possibility I'd watched them exit church together also.

Either way, they were comfortable with one another.

This realization irked me. It had me skimming my gaze over her, soaking in every inch. She was the exact opposite of me. Where I was short, she was tall. Where I had a modestly sized chest, she had melons the size of my head. My hair was brown and hers was blond. My eyes were hazel and hers were bright blue.

I zeroed in on the bronze name tag fastened to the pocket above her left breast. *Lilly.* The name clicked with her face. She was one of the Pendergrasses. They were a well-known family in Mirror Lake. Not because they had the most money, but because they owned the largest farm. A dairy farm. According to Gran, it had been in their family for generations.

"Hey, there you are." Alec smiled when I stepped to his side. "I thought you'd forgotten about me again."

"No, and I didn't forget about you the first time. I just got tied up with something."

"Well, I'm glad you're here now. I saved you a seat." He patted the stool beside him. "Did you want to grab something to eat? Fries or maybe a milkshake?"

I situated myself beside him, taking notice of how close his knee was to mine now that I was sitting. A charge zipped through the inches separating us, causing a smile to twist at the corners of my lips. I loved being close to him.

"Actually, I'm starved. I think I'm going to order a burger and fries."

"All right," he said before resting his elbows on the counter. His tone seemed off.

Had he not expected to buy me dinner when he'd offered to meet up here? It was late; maybe he didn't think dinner was an option after nine o'clock. "You don't have to buy it."

"No, it's fine. I don't mind."

"Are you sure?"

"Positive. I didn't ask you out so you could buy your own food." He winked.

Lilly cleared her throat, drawing my attention back to her. I'd forgotten she was standing there. Her blue eyes were fixed on me, and there was a pad of paper on the counter in front of her. Her pen was poised, ready to take my order. "So, you want a burger and fries?"

"Yeah, thanks," I said. Just because I didn't like the way she'd seemed so chummy with Alec didn't mean I was going to go out of my way to be mean to her. Especially not in front of him.

"And what do you want on it?" Lilly asked as she scribbled my order down with jerky movements. She didn't want to talk to me. I could sense it. Did she have a thing for Alec? Of course she did. Why else would she have been flirting with him the way she had when I walked in?

"Everything except mayo and onion."

"Anything to drink?"

I wanted the milkshake Alec had mentioned, but figured I'd better go with water instead. It would make my meal cheaper. I'd buy myself a milkshake before I left tonight, though.

"Water, please."

"And what about you? Can I get you anything?" Lilly

asked Alec. Her entire demeanor had changed now that she was speaking to him.

"I'll take some fries and a refill on my sweet tea," Alec said, oblivious to her cutesy smile.

"You got it." Lilly grinned wider as she gripped his cup and then turned to place our order.

"Sorry I'm late," I said as soon as she'd disappeared. "My Gran needed to talk to me about some family stuff." It wasn't a total lie.

Alec leaned closer. His knee brushed against mine, and I swore the area of my skin had never been more alive than it was right now.

"Everything okay?" he asked. Genuine concern flared through his brown eyes.

"Yeah, everything's fine." I leaned against the counter, careful not to move my legs so his knee would remain pressed against mine. "So, how long have you been sitting here chatting with Lilly?" I hated the way jealousy dripped from my words, but I couldn't control it. I hadn't enjoyed seeing him talking with her, and the smiles on both of their faces had killed me.

"Not long, and you don't have anything to worry about," he said as he placed a hand on my thigh. My heart kicked into overdrive at the unexpected movement. "I came here to see you, not her."

While his words were reassuring, the image of the two of them laughing would forever be burned into my memory. Normally, I'd say I wasn't the jealous type, but the situation rubbed me the wrong way. Or maybe it was the approaching full moon and what it might mean that had me looking for things to unleash my frustration and fears on.

Lilly came back with my water and Alec's sweet tea refill. She set our glasses in front of us and then shifted her attention to me. "I forgot to ask if you wanted lemon, and you didn't specify. I can get you one if you want, though."

I plastered a smile on my face just as fake as the one on hers. "No, I'm fine."

There was no way I'd ask for a lemon now. The chances of it coming from the floor were pretty high based off the look on her face. Apparently, she'd noticed Alec's hand on my thigh.

Good. She needed to know whom he belonged to.

"Your food will be out soon."

"Thanks," Alec said as she walked away. "I'm getting the impression you two don't get along."

"Your impression wouldn't be wrong," I said as I took a sip of my water, holding his gaze. His smile dimmed, and I felt myself deflate. Maybe I shouldn't have said that. "Honestly, I don't know her so I can't say for sure if I like her. What I can tell you is she doesn't like me."

"I'm sure that's not true. Lilly is really a sweet girl if you give her a chance," Alec insisted. His words seemed defensive of her in a way that made me uncomfortable. "I've known her since we were little kids. The edge of their land butts against my backyard. I used to fish out of their pond every summer and play with their animals."

He had a soft spot for her. Great. "I didn't realize you were neighbors." My words were sharp and harsh.

"Yeah, but I guess that's not helping how you feel about her, is it?" he asked as a shit-eating grin plastered on his face. Had he been trying to get a reaction out of me? Something in his eyes made me think he might have been.

"No."

Alec leaned in closer, so close I could feel his warm breath tickle my face. "That's okay. Have I ever told you I like your feisty side?"

A throaty laugh burst past my lips. He had been trying to get a reaction out of me. "Really? Well, let's just say you haven't seen my true feisty side yet."

No matter what I tossed him, he still stuck around for more. Yep, Alec Thomas was definitely a keeper.

"Alec. Hey, what's up?" a guy everyone referred to as Benji said as he reached for Alec's hand and did the weird shoulder bump thing guys always did. "We still on for Sunday?"

"Heck yeah. Right after church, meet me at my house. You can help me strap the four-wheelers to my dad's trailer and then ride to the track with me."

"He's letting you take the trailer, then? Cool," Benji said with a grin. There were remnants of something black stuck in his teeth. When he reached for a circle canister from his back pocket, I knew it was dip.

Yuck.

"It took a little convincing and some extra chores, but he eventually agreed. I just have to be careful, or he'll never let me use it again."

"That would be a bummer. It's so much easier to get them off a trailer than out of the back of a truck." Benji glanced at me, as though he'd only now noticed me. "I'll let you get back to whatever you two were doing. See you at church, man."

"See ya." Alec took a swig of his sweet tea.

"Four-wheeling?" I knew Alec was a rugged southern

boy, but I didn't realize he had a four-wheeler. I'd always wanted to ride one.

"Nothing better than slinging up some dirt after praising the almighty for a few hours."

"Um. Doesn't that contradict what you do in church?"

"Why would it?"

I took a small sip of water, thinking about what I was trying to say before I actually did. People in this town easily became offended when someone downplayed the importance of going to church. Maybe that was another reason they thought I was odd. My family didn't go to church. No one in the park did.

It wasn't that we didn't believe in God; it was that we worshiped him in a different way. Nature was our church. We didn't need fancy clothes or to be perfectly groomed to give our thanks. All we needed was a connection with the Earth.

"Well, because you're basically going to church to worship all of God's creation and thank him for it, then you leave and hop on your four-wheeler to tear it all up. It seems a bit contradictory to me," I said, watching his face, waiting for his reaction.

A lopsided grin formed. "Never thought of it that way,"

Lilly came with our food. She couldn't have picked a better time. The conversation we were having wasn't one I wanted to continue. It had the potential to veer off into something too philosophical and deep than I cared to discuss.

"Here you go. One burger, minus the onion and mayo, plus fries and another side order of fries, extra-large because that's the only way to go," Lilly said to Alec. She acted as though she'd done him a huge favor by giving him more fries than she'd charged for.

"Wow, that's a lot of fries," Alec said as he eyed the plate she'd placed in front of him.

"Oh, let me get you some ketchup. I'll be right back." She dashed toward the kitchen again.

"There's no way I can eat all of these," Alec muttered the second she was out of sight.

"I don't think many could. It looks like something from a food-eating contest. I keep waiting for her to pop-up with a timer to see if you can beat the record." I chuckled.

"I know, right? Not only that, but I ate earlier. My mom made pot roast, my favorite, and I had seconds. I feel bad she gave me so much. I know she was only trying to be nice, but I'm not that hungry."

"Then don't eat them." Seemed to be the obvious answer.

Alec leaned back, taking his hand from my thigh and moving his knee away from mine in the process. Both areas felt as though they were slowly dying from the sudden loss of contact with him. Had my words seemed too harsh? I hadn't meant them to be.

"I know, but I don't want to seem rude," he said.

Lilly came back with a bottle of ketchup. It looked brand-new. "Here you go. Let me know if you need anything else."

"Thanks, Lilly," Alec said as he picked up the bottle.

I watched her as she walked away. Her hips swayed more than they should naturally. Alec didn't seem to notice. He was still focused on the massive number of fries she'd given him.

"Hey, man," another guy from school said as he slapped

Alec on the shoulder in passing. "We still on for Sunday? Going to kick a little mud around?"

"You know it," Alec said around a mouthful of fries. "Meet at my place. We can all head out to the property together."

"Sounds good," the guy said as he continued toward the exit. His eyes drifted to me, and I swore I saw something dark reflected there. It was gone before I could name it. My gaze shifted to the tiny girl tucked into his side. She had short brown hair and doe-like eyes. She flashed me a smile, but I caught on right away it was more of a nervous gesture than something tossed out for friendship purposes.

"How many people are going four-wheeling with you on Sunday?" I asked once they were out of earshot.

"There's usually about seven of us, but a couple of the guys couldn't make it this weekend. Looks like it'll be Benji, Shane, and his girlfriend, Becca." He crammed another couple of fries into his mouth before speaking again. "Which is pretty much the usual group. Why, you want to come?"

My heart stalled. I hadn't been expecting him to invite me, but I couldn't deny how excited I was that he had. "I don't know, maybe," I said, playing it off cool. "Where are you riding them?" It didn't matter, but I felt it was a good question to ask.

"My uncle owns a little stretch of land near the lake he lets us ride on."

As long as it wasn't on Lilly's family property, I was fine with it. "Okay, sure. I'll come."

"You're serious?"

"Yeah, why wouldn't I be?"

"I don't know. Sometimes I have a hard time distinguishing when you're being serious and when you're screwing with me."

"Well, I'm definitely not screwing with you. I want to come. I've never ridden a four-wheeler before, but I've always wanted to," I admitted and then took a large bite of my burger.

"Awesome, you're going to love it. I can pick you up on my way home from church Sunday, or you can meet me at my place. Whichever is easier for you."

There was no way I wanted him to pick me up on his way home from church. He'd be dressed to impress, and everyone in the trailer park would be saying the same crap Gran was. I didn't need to hear it from anyone else that I was wasting my time with Alec, especially not when I wasn't sure I'd ever be Moon Kissed like the rest of them. I didn't have many full moons left for it to happen.

"I'll meet you at your place."

"Sounds good."

I ate the rest of my burger as Alec ate a good portion of his fries. Afterward, we ordered milkshakes to go. It wasn't until we were headed to the exit that I noticed three of Eli's brothers at a table in the corner, staring at me. I wondered how long they'd been there and why I hadn't felt their gaze before. I should have. When I was with Alec, though, nothing else mattered.

I glanced at the three of them. What were they doing here? Watching me? Their trays were empty, so maybe they'd been eating. How long had they been sitting there, though? Two of the brothers were missing from the group. There were five Vargas boys. While I was positive Eli was still at Eddie's finishing his shift, I wondered where the youngest Vargas boy was. Then again, maybe he was too young to be out and about. After all, he was only nine. Why were Tate, Cooper, and Micah here, though? This wasn't a place they frequented.

I waved at them as I passed their table with Alec at my side. Cooper and Micah acknowledged my presence with a tiny nod, but Tate flat-out ignored me. Out of these three, he was the one who reminded me of Eli most. There was something dark and serious about him the others didn't harbor.

"I know those guys are your neighbors, but they give me the creeps. That whole family does," Alec muttered once we'd stepped outside.

An uncontrollable flush of heat swept through me. Had he ever felt that way about me?

"A lot of people think that." I tasted my milkshake, trying to hide the tendrils of insecurity flickering through me.

"Do you have to be home soon?"

"No." I didn't have a curfew. Gran trusted me enough to never enforce one.

"Would you want to see the track? I know it doesn't sound cool, but it's right on the lake and I know you like the lake."

I eyed him. "How do you know that?"

"I know a lot more about you than you would think, Mina Ryan." He winked.

His words should have put me on guard. They would have if they'd come from anyone besides him. Instead, they caused delicious shivers to slip up and down my spine and my heart to beat tenfold.

Had he been watching me? Was he really that interested in me?

"Like what?" Curiosity got the best of me. There was no way Alec had watched me the way I watched him. I'd been like a hunter stalking her prey.

"You prefer to be alone rather than surrounded by people. You're stronger than you give yourself credit for because of the way you take care of your family. You don't take crap from anyone. You love the lake and the moon. And you happen to like vanilla milkshakes." He nodded to the shake in my hand as a boyish look swept across his face.

When had he learned so much about me? What made him want to?

"Have you been stalking me?" Jesus, that was the second time tonight those words had come from my mouth. However, it was the first time I'd meant them.

The only way Alec would know I liked hanging out at the lake and a few of the other things he'd mentioned was if he followed me around. A lot.

The tiny hairs on the back of my neck lifted on end.

"Not really, no," he said as he averted his gaze from mine. A pink tint splashed across his cheeks, and I knew I'd embarrassed him by putting him on the spot. "The piece of land my uncle owns connects to the lake. The section is kind of close to the trailer park where you live. Sometimes I go out there to camp, hunt, or be alone with nature. It's pretty much my favorite place in the world, and that was before I learned it was close to yours."

"Close to my what?" I wasn't following.

"Your favorite place in the world, the lake." His mouth sounded dry. He took a sip from his milkshake and then licked his lips. "I've seen you out there at night. You stare at the moon and dip your toes in the water. Sometimes it looks like you're praying or meditating or something. You look peaceful there."

My breath hitched. I hadn't realized someone had been watching me. Usually, I was in tune with my surroundings, but not lately. The last few months I'd been preoccupied. Not having been Moon Kissed yet was starting to get to me.

Generally, a person harboring the wolf gene would be Moon Kissed between their sixteenth and nineteenth birthday. I was eighteen and it hadn't happened yet. My time was running short.

"I know I sound like some sort of a creeper. I'm not, I swear," he said as he held up a hand in surrender.

"I don't think you're a creeper. I just didn't know you'd been watching me." What else had he seen? Had he seen when I skinny-dipped a few weeks ago? Had he witnessed others things in the woods he shouldn't?

"Good, I'm glad. The last thing I ever want to do is scare you away."

"You could never scare me away," I scoffed.

If anything, I would scare him away. In fact, I wasn't sure how I hadn't yet. Who did he see when he looked at me? It couldn't be the same girl everyone else saw. The one from the trailer park. The one who was different in a way that was unexplainable. Heck, it might not even be the same girl I saw when I looked in a mirror. Maybe Alec saw someone else entirely.

I was okay with that.

3

Aportion of my favorite piece of the lake happened to be on Alec's uncle's property. Apparently, I'd trespassed numerous times without realizing. This explained how he knew I enjoyed looking at the moon and visiting the lake.

The moral of the story: I needed to pay more attention to my surroundings.

We finished our milkshakes as we walked the property, heading toward the lake. Once we reached it, Alec sat and I followed suit. The night sounds surrounded us, and all the tension I'd been feeling from our lack of conversation disappeared as contentment washed over me. This lake was home.

Alec's knee brushed against mine as he better situated himself beside me. It was intentional, I could tell, but I was okay with it because I wanted to feel him too. I licked my lips and shifted to glance at him. He was staring at me with an intensity in his eyes I found surprising.

"You really love this place, don't you?" he asked.

"Yeah." The word came out as a breathy whisper.

"Everything about you seemed to relax the second we sat down."

He was so observant. I wasn't sure how I felt about it. "Tell me something about you. I feel like you already know so much about me, but I know virtually nothing about you."

It wasn't the entire truth. He hadn't been the only one watching.

I'd picked up on some things about him. I knew he had an older brother who still lived in town. His dad was a carpenter, and his mom worked at the local grocery store as a cashier. I knew his entire family had been born and raised here. He went to church every Sunday. He was a lover of sweet tea and all things barbecue, and as of tonight, I knew he enjoyed four-wheeling.

"There's not much about me you don't already know. I'm pretty much an open book," he said.

"What's your favorite type of music?" I thought I already knew, but sometimes people surprised me.

"Country."

"Well, no surprise there. That's what I would have guessed."

"See, I told you I'm an open book." He chuckled and bumped his knee into mine. "What about you? What kind of music do you like?"

"Guess."

"Okay, um. Well, I doubt you like country. On the other hand, you don't seem like the type to enjoy pop music either. Maybe rock?"

"Yeah, I'm not much of a country fan and I can't stand pop. Rock is okay, as long as it's not the hard-core, head-banging stuff. I prefer rap. There's something about the beats that really get me moving."

"Actually, I don't find that surprising at all. I've always thought of you as tough. Makes sense you'd like thuggish music."

I laughed. I'd never heard rap referred to as thuggish. It had a nice ring to it.

Something moved through the woods a few feet away. I shifted around, glancing through the brush to see what it was. Being this close to the trailer park had me thinking it might be Eli or his brother, Tate. If it were, I was going to flip out on them.

"What's wrong?" Alec asked as though he hadn't heard anything. Maybe he hadn't. Maybe my hearing was slightly better than his.

Maybe I was destined to be Moon Kissed after all.

"Nothing." I shifted back around to face the lake. "Thought I heard something."

"Probably an animal. There are all kinds of them out here, especially at night."

I held my breath, waiting for him to say something about wolves rumored to run through these woods. He didn't. This surprised me because he had to have heard the stories. His family had lived here forever.

"I'm glad we got to spend some time together tonight," Alec said.

"Yeah, me too. I'm sorry, again, for the way things have panned out. I don't want you to think I've been blowing you off. There's just been a lot going on at home." I tucked a few stray hairs behind my ear, unable to meet his gaze. Suddenly, I felt vulnerable, too vulnerable, and I didn't like it. I needed a swift change of subject. "I'm excited to go four-wheeling with you on Sunday, though. It should be fun."

"Yeah, I'm glad you wanted to come. The guys tend to be crude, just so you know, but Becca will be there. She's pretty cool. I think you'll like her."

"Was she the short girl with brown hair?"

"Yeah, she's pretty shy. You might have to give her a little while to warm up. Once she does, you can't shut her up, though."

"Noted." I chuckled. I was glad he'd told me, otherwise I might've written her off as stuck up or bitchy. Shy people often gave off those vibes for some reason.

Something crashed through the woods again behind us, garnering my attention. I glanced over my shoulder, but still didn't see anything. Whoever, or whatever it was, they weren't the most graceful. My lips pinched into a frown.

Alec shifted beside me, pulling my attention back to him. He glanced at his cell. "It's getting late. I should probably get you back to your car, unless you want me to walk you to your front door instead? My curfew is creeping up fast. If I'm not home before it, there won't be any four-wheeling this weekend."

My heart shrank two sizes at his words. "Oh, okay. I can walk home by myself, that way you're not late. My Gran can take me to my car tomorrow."

"No. I don't mind walking you home." His words were laced with a sense of earnestness, but also something else I couldn't name. Was he worried about letting me walk home through these woods alone? "There's plenty of time for that."

"All right." I stood and brushed off my bottom, hating to see my night with him end so soon. I could have sat by the lake with him for hours.

Alec scooped up his milkshake cup, and I bent to retrieve mine. A howl ripped through the night that sent cold chills sweeping through me. Was someone from the pack blowing off steam, or was it a howl of something else? I thought I'd heard panic layered in it.

"Yeah, I'm walking you home. No way would I let you go alone after hearing that," Alec insisted. He reached for my hand and interlaced his fingers through mine.

"I'm not afraid, but it is nice to have you walk me." I licked my lips, enjoying the sensation of my hand in his more than I should. Being around him made me feel good, and something that felt this good had to be right, right? Maybe this was a sign I wasn't Moon Kissed. Maybe the wolf gene would lie dormant inside me forever.

It could happen. It had before.

The question was, could I stand being on the outskirts of our pack for the rest of my life if it was never triggered? What if I was stuck as I was forever—not a human, but yet not a wolf either? I'd never fit in, no matter where I turned. I'd always be caught somewhere between.

"Don't worry. I'm not walking you because I think you're afraid," Alec said with a grin. His thumb rubbed along the top of my hand in a lazy pattern as his gaze drifted around us in a calculating way. Was he scared to be in the woods at night? Probably. We'd heard a wolf howl.

I squeezed his hand in mine as we entered a thicker part of the woods. The ground was pitted with rocks and roots, but I'd been in the woods so frequently it didn't affect me. Alec stumbled over a winding root, but righted himself before he could tumble to the ground. He let out a snort, but I didn't return it with a laugh of my own because I didn't want to embarrass him. Another howl ripped through the night. It was farther away this time. A crash followed, as though something was chasing after it.

"More distance is between us than last time. It must be moving in the opposite direction," Alec whispered.

"Yeah. I thought so too."

His grip tightened on my hand as though he was trying to reassure me. "I wouldn't let it get you, even if it wasn't."

His words were sweet, but I could hear a slight tremble waiver through them. Anyone else might not have noticed, but I did. I could sense his anxiety lingering in the air. Gran would call it my wolf intuition. I thought of it as more confirmation I wasn't normal.

I could be, though, with him. If I weren't Moon Kissed, I could be happy with Alec. Normal and happy. My intuition would always be present but nothing else. I thought of Sylvie Hess. She seemed content with the way her life had turned out even though her wolf gene had never been triggered. She'd still married and had three beautiful children within the pack. Her life had continued.

That could be me. *But would it be enough?* My subconscious asked. I didn't answer.

When we broke through the clearing of the trailer park, I steered him toward Gran's place. His body seemed to relax now that we were out of the woods. If only he knew the truth about everyone inside the park. He might not feel so safe then. The hum of Mr. Russel's air conditioner sounded as we passed by his trailer. All of his lights were off, which was normal for this time of night. He wasn't much of a night owl. In fact, he was the one who shouted for the rest of us to keep it down once seven o'clock hit.

We made our way past the Bell sisters' trailer next. Lights were on, but thankfully, I didn't see either nosy sister peeking through their blinds. A gentle gust of wind blew through the park, jostling the wind chimes the sisters hung from their porch. The noise was soothing and much better than the rapid beating of my heart filling my ears. I was worried Alec would try to kiss me while the others were watching from the shadows. While no one had come out and said it, except Gran, dating outside the pack was sort of frowned upon.

The living room light was still on when we reached my trailer. I wasn't sure if Gran had left it on in case my dad needed to get to the bathroom, or if she'd left it on for me. There was also a chance she was still awake. She'd always been a night owl. My gaze drifted over the living room windows as we paused in front of the porch stairs. Neither Gran nor Gracie seemed to be peeking out at us.

"All things considered, I had a good time tonight," I said.

"Me too," Alec insisted as he leaned forward. He pressed his lips against mine in a featherlight kiss.

My legs grew weak at the feel of his warm lips, and I found myself gripping for the front of his T-shirt to steady myself. He stepped closer and placed his hands on my hips. The plastic lid on his empty milkshake cup dug into my skin, but I ignored it, wanting nothing more than for him to remain where he was. Heat spread across my face at the sudden sensation of eyes on us. Someone was watching. I thought to break the kiss and say goodnight, but Alec's tongue skimmed across my bottom lip and every thought evaporated.

I parted my lips to allow him to deepen the kiss the way he seemed to crave, unsure which of us was more desperate for it to happen. My milkshake cup slipped from my fingers and fell to the gravel, bouncing with a hollow sound. I clasp my arms around Alec's neck and allowed myself to become lost in the taste of him on my tongue. His grip on my waist tightened, his fingers digging into my skin. My teeth scraped along his bottom lip, and I found myself going to war with a darker side of me that wanted to take over. It wanted so much more than just a sweet kiss from Alec. I raked my fingers through the hair at the base of his neck as his tongue stroked across mine, fueling the building sensations inside me. His solid body pressed against mine, and I sucked his bottom lip into the recesses of my mouth. I nipped it unintentionally. The coppery taste of blood filled my mouth as Alec jerked back, bringing his fingers to his lip.

"Ouch," he hissed. "Pretty sure you drew blood just now."

A tingling sensation swept up the back of my neck and across my face. "Sorry, I guess I got carried away."

"It's okay, I don't mind. Just surprised me is all."

I licked my lips, erasing the remnants of his blood. A compulsion to flee rushed through me at the taste, but I kept my feet rooted in place.

"I should probably go," Alec muttered. His fingertips

continued to press against his bottom lip. Had I bit him that hard? It had drawn blood, but I didn't think it was a gaping wound. "As it is I'm probably going to be cutting it close to curfew anyway." He dropped his hand to his side and flashed me a small smile I could barely make out in the moonlight.

"I can't wait for Sunday," I said, because I didn't know what else to say. There was an awkward tension building between us. "I won't get sidetracked or anything either. I'll totally meet you at your house in the afternoon."

"Good, I'll be waiting." He winked before walking away.

I watched him until he disappeared from my view between Mr. Russel's trailer and old man Winter's. A long sigh escaped me as I took a step toward the stairs of our front porch.

"I wouldn't have been such a wimp if you bit me, just so you know," a familiar voice said from somewhere in the shadows.

I spun around to spot Eli at the edge of his family's trailer. He held a large cardboard box in his arms, and there was a wicked grin twisted onto his face. Now I knew who'd been watching us.

I folded my arms over my chest. "One, I wouldn't kiss you, let alone bite you. And two, Alec didn't act like a wimp. He just had to get home before curfew."

Eli balanced the cardboard box he'd been holding on the bumper of his truck. His eyes never wavered from mine, and the devilish grin on his face only intensified. "Are you kidding me? The kid looked like you attacked him."

"He did not." Did he? He had seemed shocked, but wouldn't anyone?

"Yeah, I think he did. Why else do you think he ran away so damn fast?"

"Like I said, he didn't want to be late for his curfew."

Eli shook his head. "Because that's what every guy is worried about while lip-locking with a hottie."

"Whatever, it's none of your business anyway. You shouldn't have been spying on me." Thoughts of Tate and his other brothers at the diner flashed through my mind. "And you shouldn't have your brothers do it either."

"No one is spying on you, least of all me. Looking out for you, yeah. Spying, no."

"Who said I needed you, or anyone else, to look out for me?"

"No one, but it doesn't mean we aren't going to do it anyway. Especially when you're dating that boy," Eli growled. He picked up the cardboard box he'd been holding and walked away.

"Stop calling him *that boy*. His name is Alec!" I shouted after him, enjoying the fact I'd gotten the last word.

"I'll stop calling him that when you stop dating him," Eli called over his shoulder.

"Not going to happen, so you better get used to speaking his name."

"Oh, it will happen, trust me," I heard him say before he stepped to old man Winter's trailer. He started up the cinderblock stairs and disappeared inside.

Eli might have gotten the last word, but it was because I'd been surprised to see him enter old man Winter's trailer. That trailer had been vacant for nearly three years. Mr. Winter had been in his seventies when he left. Or vanished.

Whichever way you wanted to look at it, he was no longer in the park, the pack, or the town.

Some claimed the old guy knew his time was coming and wandered into the woods to be one with the moon for a final time. Some say he'd gotten sick of this town and its people, so he joined a new pack or became a solitary wolf. No one knew what actually happened to the old man, and I doubted anyone cared. He wasn't the nicest guy. Maybe we were better off without him.

It had taken a year and a half before Bobby, the guy who owned the park, cleaned out all of Mr. Winter's things. Some of the pack members had been pissed, but I understood his reasoning. This park was his only source of income. He had to clean the place so he could rent it again. Especially considering the condition old man Winter had left it in. He was the worst hoarder I'd ever seen. At the time he left, it had probably been years since he'd thrown a single thing away.

A light came on inside Mr. Winter's trailer. It allowed me to see Eli clearly. He was in the kitchen. I watched as he set the cardboard box that he'd been carrying on the counter. He glanced around, and I wondered if he was moving in.

Had Eli finally moved out on his own?

He was twenty-one, so it was about damn time, but I still found myself shocked by the prospect of it. I folded my arms over my chest and continued staring at him through the window. When he reached inside the cardboard box he'd carried in and pulled out a mason jar filled with a clear liquid I knew wasn't water, I grinned. He twisted the cap off and put the jar to his lips.

Yeah, Eli looked right at home. My grin grew. I was happy for him.

When he set the jar on the counter and shifted to face me, my heart thundered inside my chest. Had he felt me watching him? A lopsided grin formed on his face. He crooked his finger, beckoning me to come to him. Heat bloomed through my lower stomach as my heart rate spiked even higher. Before I could think of slipping inside my trailer as though I hadn't been spotted, my feet moved toward Eli Vargas.

4

The front door to the trailer opened before I could start up the cinderblock stairs. Eli stood in the threshold, his body taking up the entirety of its space as he looked down at me. I held his gaze, knowing I shouldn't be here but unable to make myself turn around and head home.

"You surprised me," Eli muttered in a deep, rich timbre that sent warmth streaking through my lower belly.

"Why?"

"I didn't think you'd have it in you to come over."

I didn't either, but here I was, standing at his doorstep. Eli's eyes narrowed playfully, causing my mouth to go dry. I shouldn't be here. What was I doing?

"Must've been the prospect of drinking a little moonshine that enticed you," he said with a wink.

"Maybe," I heard myself say even though I knew it wasn't true. We both did.

Alcohol wasn't my thing. Granted, I'd only drank a

handful of times—the majority of them being forced upon me by Gran who was a firm believer in whiskey as a go-to remedy for any cough or cold—but it had never appealed to me the way it did others. I couldn't stand the taste or smell. Maybe it was because of my dad. Seeing him destroy his life one sip at a time was enough of a deterrent.

Eli arched a brow. "Really? Well, you're more than welcome to a sip." He stepped to the side, allowing me room to slip past him if I wanted. "But I figured it was curiosity that had you walking over here."

I didn't confirm or deny either. Instead, I started up the steps to slip past him. The cinderblocks swayed beneath my feet, making me feel off-balanced enough to reach out. I gripped Eli's forearm to steady myself. Electricity zinged through my fingertips and up my arm at the contact. "I, um, think one of your blocks might be out of place. They feel wobbly."

"It's on my list of repairs," he said, his gaze dipping to where I touched him. Could he feel an electrical current pulsing along his skin, too?

I didn't study his reaction long enough to see. Instead, I released my grip on him and stepped farther into the trailer, placing distance between us. My hands crammed into the back pockets of my jeans as I forced myself to look around. There wasn't much to see. A couple of cardboard boxes, some blankets, and a large duffle bag.

"So, did you buy this place, or are you renting it from Bobby?" I started across the sticky linoleum floor, heading for the kitchen. It seemed far enough away from him, but not enough to be noticed as intentional.

"Why are you so interested?"

"I'm not." I'd spoken too quickly. It made my words sound defensive. I risked a glance at Eli. He'd closed the trailer door and stood staring at me with his arms folded across his chest. Suspicion glinted in the bright green of his eyes. "I didn't think this place would ever be rented out again is all. Bobby's tried for years but not gotten any bites."

I knew why. We all did. While Bobby might own the place, the pack decided when someone new moved in. More specifically Eli's dad. He was our Alpha.

The place had sat vacant because no new wolves had found their way to Mirror Lake looking for a new home, and we didn't allow humans to live here. We didn't need someone figuring out what his or her neighbors were and freaking out. Bobby knew what we were and he was fine with it, but only because he had a secret of his own. There were a lot of people living in Mirror Lake who did.

"Yeah, I know. Hence why the place is falling apart." Eli motioned to the trailer as a whole.

It wasn't in the best condition, but it was still livable.

"You can't blame him; the guy is old. He's got to be in his sixties at least. I can't imagine him fixing this place up on his own. Cut him some slack," I insisted.

Bobby was a decent guy. He'd slashed the rent on our trailer after my dad's accident to make things easier on our family. If he hadn't, I wasn't sure how we'd make it. Dad was on disability, but it wasn't enough to live on. Not with Gracie and me to care for. Mom had worked when she was still around, which helped, but since she left, the slack had fallen to Gran. Granted Gran had always run her herbal remedy store from our kitchen, but she mostly serviced the pack and none of them were ever in much need for her remedies. It was her retirement accounts that kept food in our stomachs.

I'd offered to get a job, but Gran wouldn't allow me to. Babysitting for some of the pack kids was about all she was willing to let me do because it helped those in our pack. Now that graduation was over, I had hoped she'd allow me to get a real job and help more. It was still to be determined. She was pressing me to go to the community college, which would mean the same rule for a job would apply. If I was in school, she didn't want me working; she wanted me focusing on my studies. I still hadn't decided if I'd be enrolling in the fall. I didn't know what I wanted to do with my life. All I knew was that I wanted to relish this summer, celebrating the fact I'd survived high school first.

"Which is why I worked out a deal with him," Eli said, snapping my attention back to him. "If I fix the place up, he knocks off some of the rent each month. Helps us both out. Bobby gets his place spiffed up, and I get a discount on rent. Win-win."

"That's a decent deal, but wouldn't it be easier to rent one of the vacant lots and put your own trailer on it?" Living in a junker had to be frustrating. Did the plumbing even work? The place had sat for so long it had to be questionable.

"Too expensive."

"You could get a roommate, or you could ask Dorian to rent out his trailer. Since he moved in with Sheila, he's not been staying there. No one has. And everyone knows they're not going to break up anytime soon. They're so lovesick with each other they make me want to puke every time I see them."

"Are you offering to be my roommate?" Eli's lips hooked

in a half grin. He obviously heard nothing beyond the word roommate.

"No, I'm just saying it might be a better option than having to fix up this place." I forced myself to look away from him. He was sucking me in with his eyes the way he always did. I hated the sensation of not being in control of my body when I was around him; if I continued to stare into his gorgeously colored eyes, that's right where I was going to be.

"I don't mind fixing the place up. It helps me and Bobby."

Eli always had been a hard worker. It was something his father had instilled in him.

"There's not much to fix right away. The stairs are at the top of my list, next comes the rotted-out floorboard beneath that window," he said as he pointed to the window in the space I remembered Mr. Winter used to have a small dining room table. "There's a leak. Every time it rains, water seeps from the window onto the floor. Shouldn't be too hard to fix, though."

He moved into the kitchen, walking right up to me, and reached around me for the mason jar of moonshine on the counter. His silver chain glistened in the fluorescent light of the kitchen as it dangled from his neck, and his masculine scent wafted to my nose. I reached out and gripped the counter, steadying myself.

"Just grabbing this," he whispered. His hot breath tickled my neck. "It's apple pie. You'll probably like it."

He took a step back, placing the distance my mind craved but my body wanted to reject between us. I watched as Eli twisted the lid off the jar, the muscles of his arm bulging, and took a long swig. The corners of his eyes creased, but he didn't seem as though the moonshine tasted horrible. He held the jar out to me. I could smell the stoutness of it in the air.

My nose wrinkled. "Apple pie? I doubt it tastes like it."

"Maybe not exactly, but it's still sweet and there is a hint of apple." He brought the jar closer to me.

I took it from him and put it to my lips. Sweet battery acid dripped down my throat as I forced myself to swallow a big gulp. My eyes squinted shut as each intake of air flamed the fire coursing down my throat. I broke out into a coughing fit and heard Eli laugh.

"Jesus, I only expected you to take a small sip. Not down it like freaking water."

I wiped my mouth with the back of my hand, still unable to talk, and made a slight choking noise.

"Let's see how you handle that before you drink anymore." He took the jar from me and placed it to his lips. How did he not look like he was dying afterward? He didn't even cough.

"I wasn't planning on drinking anymore," I managed to choke out.

"Good, because I wouldn't let you even if you wanted to."

A part of me wanted to grab the jar from him and take another sip to prove he didn't get to dictate what I did and didn't do, but I couldn't make myself do it. Mainly because I didn't think I could handle another sip of the liquid fire. I might die.

"Did you end up having a good night overall? I saw how it ended, and I know how it began. How was the middle?" Eli asked as he twisted the lid back on the mason jar. He tucked it into the cabinet above the stove and shifted to face me fully.

"I did," I muttered unsure why he cared to ask.

"Did you manage to get your dad inside all right? I should've called Tate to come over and help."

The warmth of the moonshine moved toward my stomach and the fire burning up my esophagus dimmed the more saliva I swallowed. "I managed."

"I don't doubt you did. All I'm saying is Tate could have helped you." Eli leaned against the counter. His bright green eyes locked with mine, and I noticed a softness shift through them. "I promise, next time, I won't serve him so much alcohol, but I can't promise I won't call you again to come get him."

"Thanks," I whispered. A warm fuzzy sensation built in my stomach before sweeping through my body. I wasn't sure if I was feeling grateful toward Eli for what he'd said he'd do, or if it had something to do with the battery acid I'd drank.

"No problem. I figured if the shoe was on the other foot, you'd do the same for me." The sweetness of his words hit me hard. The warmth I'd been feeling intensified tenfold.

It had to be the alcohol.

Or maybe it was Eli? He was too close to me in the tiny kitchen. And we were alone. Utterly alone. My chest ballooned with heat as I realized this. I was too hot and slightly dizzy. I forced my eyes away from him and wiped my brow. Eli laughed.

"What's so funny?" My words sounded distorted, as if I were underwater.

"You. You're such a damn lightweight, Mina."

I forced myself to stand straighter. "I don't drink. Ever. And besides, most guys would be happy to hang out with a cheap drunk, wouldn't they?"

"Never said I wasn't happy about it."

His words sent my heart racing. My eyes zeroed in on his lips, and all I could think about was what it would feel like to kiss him. My head spun at the thought. This was Eli I was thinking about. Eli Vargas. He was mysterious and put off dangerous vibes. He was older than me, and oh dear God, he was hot.

I allowed my gaze to drift over his perfect features, taking in his dark, short-cropped hair, baby smooth face, beautiful eyes with lashes so dark and long I wanted to touch them to see if they were real, and plump, kissable lips. The strange pull I always seemed to feel toward him tugged at me.

No! I couldn't allow myself to give into whatever I was feeling. I couldn't allow myself to give into him.

I licked my lips and averted my gaze, as much as it hurt me to do so, and checked out the kitchen again. It became interesting as I forced myself to soak in its details. It was old and dated, but still functional. It had everything you'd expect: refrigerator, stove, sink, and a dishwasher. There were plenty of cabinets to store stuff in, although some of them were missing handles, and there was loads of counter space. The walls looked as though they'd been painted white at one time, but now were more of a yellow due to years of nicotine build up. The cabinets were dark brown and the countertops a shade lighter than the walls. The sticky linoleum I'd encountered when I first walked through the front door traveled into the kitchen as well. It looked as though it used to be white with black squares, but the white squares had long ago been stained yellow.

"Does it meet your standards?" Eli asked. His eyes were on me, I could feel them, but I refused to look at him. There was no telling what I'd do if I allowed myself a single glance.

"It's functional," I said as I moved toward the living room.

The trailer held an open floor plan. While this wasn't the first time I'd been inside old man Winter's place, it had been a while. The summer before he went to meet his maker, or whatever had happened to him, he'd hired me to clean out some of the mess he'd accumulated. It hadn't been a pretty picture, but then again, I hadn't expected one. I'd known he was a hoarder. Everyone did.

"That it is," Eli said from behind me. He was closer than I'd thought. I could feel his warm breath on the back of my neck. Energy pulsed between the few inches of space separating us. "It's a little bare in here, but I'll have it fixed up and looking like home in no time."

"I'm sure," I said, focusing on his presence. He took a step closer and reached out as though to brush along my forearm. I dodged his touch. "I should probably head home. Thanks for the...um...drink."

"Yeah, sure. No problem. Maybe next time you swing by I'll have furniture." He grinned and smoothed a hand over his short-cropped hair.

I didn't respond. Instead I bolted for the door.

My shoes crunched against the loose gravel that connected each trailer like a web as I made my way back to my place. Eli was watching me through his windows; I could feel the heat of his gaze traveling over my backside, but I didn't look back. I wasn't sure what had happened back there, but I was all for blaming it on the damn moonshine.

It had intensified the pull I felt to him and had me feeling things for him I'd never experienced before.

It couldn't happen again. I wouldn't let it.

The same distance I'd always placed between us would continue to be there. I would make sure of it.

My heart pounded as I crept up the wooden steps to my front door. When I slipped inside, the scent of chamomile and lemon balm tickled my nose. Gran was in her recliner, sipping a steaming mug of tea while reading a book.

"What are you still doing up?" I asked as I carefully closed the door behind me. Dad was still passed out on the couch, snoring. It wasn't him I was concerned about waking, though. It was Gracie.

"Waiting for you to get home," Gran said as she flipped the page of her book without looking up at me.

"You didn't have to." Guilt flickered through me.

"I wanted to." Her dull blue eyes skimmed over me, giving me a once-over. I hated when she did that. It always felt as though she could see more than surface level, as if she could see directly into my soul. "Feeling a little torn, aren't you?"

"Torn?" Why would she think I was feeling torn? Was that what she'd called buzzed in her day? Because that was all I was feeling. The alcohol was still coursing through my system.

"No need to play dumb, child. I can sense it about you. Your emotions are off. Confusion saturates the air around you." Her eyes glossed over as she continued to stare at me. If I hadn't already known Gran was Moon Kissed, I would've thought she was a witch. She always swore it was sharp intuition that coursed through her. Some days I wondered. "I told you hanging around that boy wasn't going to do you any good. You're only kidding yourself, Mina."

I rolled my eyes. This again. "He has a name."

"His name is no matter to me. The more you hang out with him, the more confused you're going to become. Especially after you become Moon Kissed. You're setting yourself up for hardship, dear."

"And what if that never happens? What if I never become Moon Kissed? What then?" I knew I should hold my tongue, especially when speaking to Gran, but I found it impossible. The liquid fire I'd had with Eli was giving me the courage to speak my mind.

"It will. I can sense it about you."

"Really? Could you sense it about Sylvie, too? If so, you should have mentioned it to her. Maybe then she would've moved on instead of settling down with someone from the pack."

"It doesn't work like that. You're family, which is why I can sense it in you." Gran sounded so sure of herself chill bumps spread across my skin.

I wondered if that was how it worked. Had Sylvie's family felt she wouldn't be a true part of the pack? Had they known she wouldn't be Moon Kissed?

"Hanging around that boy and Eli is only going to tear you apart, Mina. Eventually, you'll have to choose which you prefer—man or wolf—because you won't be able to hold on to both," Gran said before she opened her book to the page she'd left off on, dismissing me.

I made my way down the hall toward the bedroom Gracie and I shared, still able to feel the warmth of Eli's apple pie moonshine coursing through my system while Gran's words buzzed through my head. Would there come a day when I had to choose between them? Why?

Once I reached my bedroom, I crept inside and slipped

off my shoes. The soft sounds of Gracie sleeping floated to my ears. I peeled off my skinny jeans and tugged my hair free from its ponytail. My pillow called to me. It had been one hell of a night. I crawled into bed and pulled my sheet over me, kicking my thicker blanket to the end of the bed.

Gran's words repeated through my mind, and I pondered which guy I felt pulled to more—Alec or Eli, man or wolf?

5

I waited until a little after one on Sunday before I sent Alec a text asking if church was over yet. It didn't take long for him to respond telling me it had been out for nearly an hour.

Don't worry, though. I just got to my house ten minutes ago. My dad was starved and decided to swing by a burger joint for lunch before heading home.

That made me feel better. At least he wasn't sitting at his house, waiting on me.

Okay, so should I head over now? - Mina

Yeah, I'm changing really quickly, and then I'll head out to load the four-wheeler on the trailer. Benji should be here soon, too.

On my way. - Mina

Make sure you wear something you don't mind getting dirty. Jeans are always best.

I never mind getting dirty. I think I'll be okay. - Mina

I realized the innuendo someone could find in my words and my face heated.

You're always down for getting dirty. Good to know.

My stomach flip-flopped. I didn't know what to say in response, so I said nothing. Instead, I tossed my phone onto my bed and went to the dresser to see if I could find an old pair of jeans. The short shorts I'd put on earlier weren't going to cut it. I pulled on an old pair of jeans and struggled with the button. They were tight but would have to do.

"Where are you going? And why are you wearing jeans? It's like eighty-five out," Gracie said as she barreled into the room.

"Out with Alec. We're meeting some of his friends and going four-wheeling," I said as I finally fastened the button.

Gracie rolled her eyes. "Four-wheeling, really?"

"Yeah, I think it'll be fun." I shrugged.

"Whatever, it's too hot to be outside. You're going to melt in jeans. Besides, I thought Gran warned you not to hang out with that Alec guy anymore."

"I don't mind the heat. I'm not going to melt. And Gran never told me I couldn't hang out with him. She only said she didn't *like* me hanging out with him so much." My mind flashed back to what she'd said about having to choose between man and wolf soon. A shiver slipped along my spine.

Gracie flopped down on her bed and reached for the paperback she'd been reading. It was a paranormal romance novel with a girl and a guy on the cover almost kissing. She enjoyed everything paranormal, as though our day-to-day lives didn't have enough of it for her already.

"Same difference," Gracie snapped. "I don't see why you're spending so much time with him either. Not when you could be spending all your time with Eli Vargas." Her brows wiggled up and down in a suggestive manner.

My heart rate increased at the mention of his name. "Why would I spend all my time with Eli Vargas?"

"Why not? He's gorgeous. He's Moon Kissed. He's the Alpha's son. And he's definitely got the hots for you. Bonus, he's got his own place now."

How did she know he had the hots for me? Better yet, how did she know he'd gotten his own place? I'd only just found out, and it had been by chance. "Mind your own business, Gracie."

"You know I'm right on all levels."

I didn't respond. Instead, I reached for a hair tie off the top of our shared dresser and pulled my hair into a ponytail.

"Fine, ignore me. Ignore Gran. See if I care." She fluffed her pillows and made herself comfortable on her bed. "By the way, Eli is in our living room. See if you can ignore him on your way out the door for your date with Alec."

"What? Why is Eli in our living room?"

Gracie didn't say anything, giving me a taste of my own medicine. Her lips twisted into a smirk as she focused on the pages of her paperback. I held my breath, listening for Eli's voice. Only low murmurings made their way to my ears. I couldn't distinguish any words. My steps were slow and cautious as I made my way down the hall toward the living room. Gran was talking to someone, but I wasn't sure who. Not until I was close enough to hear him reply.

"Thanks, Mrs. Ryan," Eli said. I could tell it was him by the rich timbre of his voice. "I don't have a whole lot for the place yet. Especially not pots and pans, so this should come in handy."

I crept down the hall, pulled by the sound of his voice. It stirred butterflies awake in the pit of my stomach.

"You'll get settled in soon. These things take time. Now, remember what I said about that pan," Gran insisted. "You have to make sure you grease it after each use. If you plan on washing it, that is."

"You don't wash yours?"

"Not if I don't have to. Things taste better when they're cooked in a seasoned skillet."

"Then maybe I won't wash mine either."

I paused at the end of the hall, still slightly hidden. Eli was on the couch and Gran was in her recliner. Dad was nowhere to be seen, and I found myself wondering if he'd already started his daily binge at the bar.

"Then you have to continue to cook the same thing in it. It can't be used for anything else. The one I don't wash I use to cook sausage in."

Eli made a disgusted face that had me cupping my hands over my mouth to keep my laughter in. It was exactly how I felt about it. I'd always thought never washing the pan was disgusting. It was a wonder no one had gotten sick over the years when eating Gran's sausage.

"Never? You've never washed the pan you cook sausage in?"

"Once a year. That's it."

Eli pursed his lips together and smoothed a hand along the top of his head. "Huh, okay."

"You going to come join the conversation or continue to eavesdrop from the hall?" Gran asked, surprising me.

"I wasn't eavesdropping," I said as I stepped forward, trying to appear calmer than what I felt from having been busted.

"What would you call standing in the hallway listening to a conversation you're not part of, then?" she asked with an arched brow. I didn't say anything, because what could I? She knew what I'd been doing.

"Afternoon, Mina," Eli greeted me. The way his lips curled over the letters of my name had my knees going weak.

"Hi," I said with a small smile before shifting my attention to Gran. "I'm headed out. I'll be back before dinner, though."

"You better be. I'm making your favorite, pork chops and black-eyed peas with greens."

"Sounds good," I said as I slinked out our front door. "See you later."

"I should probably get going too," I heard Eli say before the door had even closed behind me. "Thanks again for the skillet. I'll be sure I put it to good use."

"You're welcome. Let me know if there's anything else you need."

"Thanks," Eli said as he bolted out the door. In seconds, he was right on my heels. I could feel the heat of his eyes scorching my backside as I dug my keys out of my purse. "Isn't it a little hot for jeans?"

"I don't mind the heat."

"Never said you did."

I didn't look at him. Looking into his eyes was a risk I wasn't taking. I knew I'd get sucked into their crazy color. Too much time would pass and I'd end up leaving Alec hanging again. I couldn't do that. The afternoon involved his friends, and I wanted to make a good impression on them. Heck, I wanted to erase the one they'd had of me since birth and replace it with something good.

I found my keys and opened my driver side door. The entire car shook as the latch undid.

"You should swing by my place later tonight," Eli said.

I froze. My eyes lifted to his. "Why?"

"To see what I've done with the place since Friday. It's a little homier than before." He shifted the cast iron pan around in his hands as a wide grin sprang onto his face. "And now that I have this nifty skillet, I can whip us up something to eat so the moonshine doesn't affect you as much the second time around."

I swallowed hard. Where did he get off inviting me over for dinner and a drink? Was Gracie right? Did he have the hots for me?

It didn't matter. I was with Alec. Sort of. At least I was working on being with him.

"I don't think so. Thanks for the offer, though."

"It's freestanding," Eli insisted as he walked away from me backward, his grin never dimming.

"Thanks, but no thanks." I slipped behind the wheel and cranked the engine, closing the door without glancing at Eli again.

Alec. I was going to meet Alec.

My eyes flicked to the clock on my dash. Too much time had already passed. I should be there by now.

Gravel crunched beneath my tires as I pulled out of my parking space, making my way to the main road. I caught sight of Eli's back as I drove. His skin glinted in the sunlight, and his muscles flexed and bulged as he swung his arms while he walked. My gaze drifted ahead of him toward old man Winter's trailer. Something was different. It only took me a second to figure out what.

The cinderblock stairs were gone.

In their place stood a set of beautifully crafted wooden ones. A tentative smile twisted my lips. He'd moved fast on that project. If he'd already changed the stairs, what else had he done to the place? Curiosity simmered through my veins. Not knowing was going to eat at me.

Even so, I wasn't visiting Eli again. Not tonight. Not ever if I could help it.

6

Alec's house was about twenty minutes from mine. He lived on the opposite side of town. I'd been to his home once before, so it wasn't hard to find. He'd gotten a call from his mom on his way to pick me up the first time we decided to hang out. She'd needed milk for a recipe she was making. To this day, I suspected she hadn't needed the milk, but instead wanted to see whom he was with.

She'd been decent to me when I met her, but it had also been clear she knew where I came from and didn't like it. The second I'd offered my last name, her entire demeanor had changed. I knew it was because she didn't want me hanging around her son. Alec hadn't seemed to catch on, though. If he had, he was good at hiding it and okay with going against her wishes, considering we were still hanging out weeks later.

Nervous butterflies broke out in flight in the pit of my stomach as I rounded the final corner before Alec's house.

His place was coming up on the left. Even if I hadn't remembered, the vehicles parked in his driveway would have tipped me off. Both Shane and Benji were here, which meant I was late.

I pulled in behind a silver truck and noticed someone sitting inside. It had to be Becca.

I debated if I should cut my engine since I'd probably have to move my car in a second anyway. It dawned on me then that I should have opted to meet Alec at the track. It was beside my place anyway. Would have saved me gas, and no one would have had to wait around on me. I wished I'd thought of that before.

Screw it. I was here now. There was no going back.

I cut the engine on my car and climbed out. My tank top stuck to me in places as I made my way to where Becca sat in the cab of the silver truck. Gracie was right. I was probably going to melt in these jeans.

"Strap that one down tighter," I heard Alec say. "I don't want it to slip off when I go around a corner."

"There, that good?" Benji asked. I recognized his voice clearly. His words always sounded muffled from the dip in his mouth, and he had a slightly more southern accent than the other guy had.

"Yeah, that should do. As soon as Mina gets here, we can leave," Alec said. He didn't sound agitated, but I doubted he enjoyed waiting around on me.

"I can't believe you invited her," the other guy said. Shane. His name had been Shane.

"Why?" Alec asked. The defensive tone to his words warmed me. It wasn't that I wanted him to butt heads with his friends because of me, but it was nice to know he was down to stick up for me if need be.

"She's weird, man."

"She's not weird," Benji said, surprising me. "She's freakin' hot."

"Watch yourself," Alec said. I could hear a smirk in his tone.

"Just sayin'."

"Whatever. There's something weird about her. I'm telling you. There's something weird about everyone in that trailer park," Shane insisted, causing my heart to thunder in my chest.

"You've been listenin' to the old timers way too much, dude. There's nothin' wrong with the people who live in the trailer park," Benji said.

"Sorry about Shane," Becca whispered as she leaned her head out the window and eyed me. Her cheeks were pink. I wasn't sure if it was from the heat, or because of what her boyfriend had said. "He's the one who can be weird sometimes."

I hated that she felt a need to apologize for him. No one should. Not because I felt he should own up to what he was saying, but because he was right. There was something weird about those of us who lived in the trailer park, and out of the four of them, he was the only one smart enough to realize it and listen.

"It's fine," I said with a shrug.

A light breeze blew, sending hot air blowing around me. I wished I'd kept my shorts on.

Becca tucked a few stray strands of hair behind her ear

and flashed me a shy smile. "Anyway, I'm glad you're coming today."

"Really?" Was she screwing with me or being serious? It was hard to tell.

"Yeah, I mean it's always fun watching the guys horse around on the track, but it can be boring when they do it every weekend."

"You just watch? You don't ride with them?" What was the point in going if you weren't going to ride?

She shook her head. "No. I just watch."

"What's the fun in that?"

"I don't know. I mean, I rode on the back of Shane's a couple of times before, but that's about it."

"You should drive one today."

Her doe-like eyes widened. "No way! Shane would never let me drive."

"Why not? I don't see what the big deal is."

"That four-wheeler is his baby. So is this truck," Becca said.

"What you're saying is he's never let you drive his truck either?" The guy sounded like a real ass.

"God, no."

"Well, from what you just told me about him, it doesn't seem like he's much fun."

"He is. He's just..."

"Weird?" I offered with a wicked smirk.

Becca laughed. "Yeah, definitely."

My smirk widened. I had a feeling I'd enjoy hanging out with Becca today. She might be shy, but inside resided a girl who wanted to have fun. I could sense it, and I was going to make sure I found a way to let that girl out today.

"Hey, there you are," Alec said, drawing my attention to him. He flashed me a large smile.

"Yup, here I am. I didn't mean to keep you guys waiting." I flashed the guys a little wave. Benji was the only one who returned it. Shane flat-out ignored me.

"You didn't keep us waiting. We had a hard time getting the four-wheelers on the trailer," Alec said. "Now that they're strapped in and you're here, you ready to head out?"

"Yeah, sure. Let me back my car out so everyone can get out." I hitched my thumb over my shoulder and started walking backward.

"Just pull it in the grass," Alec insisted.

"Are you sure? It'll only take me a second to get out of everyone's way."

"Nah, it's fine."

"I don't want your parents pissed at me for ruining their grass." They didn't need another reason to dislike me, especially his mom.

"They won't be." Alec laughed. "Seriously, just pull it in the grass and get in my truck." A wiry hint of a smile curled the corners of his mouth. He seemed to like bossing me around in a flirty tone. I didn't mind.

After I moved my car to the grass, I headed to Alec's truck. He was already positioned behind the wheel, engine cranked, and Benji leaned against the passenger door. He was waiting for me to get in so he could sandwich me between the two of them.

"You ever rode one before?" Benji asked as I slipped into the cab and scooted across the leather seat.

It was a good thing I hadn't worn shorts. Humid temperatures and leather seats were not a good combination for bare legs.

"Nope, this will be my first time," I said.

"You serious?" Benji asked as he slipped in the cab beside me and closed the door. He reached for a plastic bottle on the floorboard I'd somehow missed when climbing in and placed it to his lips. Brown liquid oozed from his mouth and congregated inside the bottle.

"Yeah." My upper lip curled. "And that is seriously disgusting."

"This?" One of Benji's bushy eyebrows raised as amusement flitted across his face. "Hang around me enough and you'll get used to it."

"He's right," Alec offered. "You will."

"You don't dip, do you?" I'd never noticed Alec having gunk stuck in his teeth or a fat lip from a wad of the crap crammed between his gums and his teeth, but I knew that didn't mean anything.

"Me?" Alec popped his truck into reverse and crept out of his driveway. "No way. My momma would kill me."

Thank goodness. I didn't think I could handle seeing him spit nasty brown crap in a bottle all day, too.

"Woo wee, this is gonna be fun," Benji chimed as he rolled down his window and smacked his hand on the side of the truck.

"Damn right," Alec said, flashing me a tiny grin as he shifted into drive.

Adrenaline rushed through me. I had a feeling today was going to be fun, regardless of Shane and his obvious dislike of me. I could ignore him. Heck, I ignored people all the time. He would be no different.

I STOOD at the back of Alec's truck, watching as he helped the guys get their four-wheelers off the trailer. The lean muscles in his arms flexed as he pulled and jerked the big pieces of machinery. Beads of sweat built across his brow, and his cotton T-shirt seemed to stick to him in places. Part of me wished he'd go ahead and shed the shirt. It would help with the heat and give me a view of the abs I'd felt the other night when he'd kissed me goodbye.

"Let me take a quick ride around the track to make sure it's free of branches from the last storm before everyone rides out," Alec insisted. He climbed on his four-wheeler and revved its engine to life. Did he always act so by the book with everything? He'd never seemed like a safety-first kind of guy until now. "It'll take me a second. When I get back, I'll give you a ride," Alec shouted over the rumble of his engine to me.

I nodded and flashed him a smile, watching as he started around the track.

"I'm sure he wants to give you a ride all right." Benji nudged my shoulder.

I laughed. I couldn't help it. The guy was turning out to be quite the character.

"Mina, do you want a bottle of water?" Becca asked from where she sat on Shane's tailgate.

"Yeah, sure. Thanks," I said as I made my way toward her. My mouth was super dry.

Becca pulled a cooler to her and flipped the top up. She reached in and dug around, searching for a bottle. When she found one, she wiped away a few pieces of ice stuck to its sides and handed it to me.

"We can sit over there in the shade if you want. That's normally where I sit," she said as she pointed behind me and then jumped down from Shane's tailgate.

"For a little while, but I'm not planning on sitting there all afternoon and neither are you." I flashed her a pointed look while I twisted open my water.

"What's that supposed to mean?" Shane asked. I didn't care for the hostility in his words.

"Becca isn't sitting out this time. I'm going to get her on the back of one of those things today," I said as I nudged her shoulder with mine. "Then I'm going to get her to drive one."

"Yeah, I don't think so," Shane scoffed.

Wow, I'd thought he'd be happy she wanted to participate. "Why do you say that?"

"Um, because Becca has only ridden one a couple of times. There's no way in hell I'm letting her drive mine."

"Who said it has to be yours?" I asked. There were two other four-wheelers here, and I doubted either of their owners would oppose to sharing. Unlike him.

"Oh, man. She got you." Benji chuckled from where he sat on his four-wheeler, waiting for Alec to come back with an all clear.

Shane pressed his lips together in a way that emphasized his jaw. His eyes narrowed on me, but I didn't look away. He didn't intimidate me. Once he figured that out, he hopped on his four-wheeler and started the engine. His gaze flicked to Becca, and I was pleased to see she held his stare dead on instead of looking away like I'd expected. Maybe she had more backbone than I gave her credit for.

"Come on, let's get in the shade. We've only been out here a few minutes and I'm already burning up," Becca said. She started walking, opening her water as she went.

"I'm sorry, but Shane is an ass. I don't know why you're even with him," I muttered once we were away from the guys.

We eased into the shady area, and I swore there was a ten-degree difference. No wonder she was content to sit here all day while the guys rode around on their toys.

"He's not always like that," Becca insisted. "I think he got his man feelings hurt just now or something."

I started to say maybe it was my presence bringing out the worst in him, but bit my tongue instead. While I liked Becca, I still didn't know her well, and I wasn't about to continue to beat a dead horse. She knew I thought her boyfriend had asshole-ish tendencies. That was enough for now.

I took a sip of my water and spotted Alec on his way back around the track. He wore a calculated look on his face as he crept forward at a snail's pace.

"Is he always that serious?" I asked Becca.

"Only the first time around the track. After that, he loosens up."

I sat down in the grass. "So, what do you normally do while they goof off on the track? Sit in the shade and watch?"

"Sometimes." She shrugged. "Sometimes I bring a book or do my homework. The cell phone reception sucks out here, so I can't cruise the Internet for anything."

"Oh my God, that sounds so boring." I hung my head back and glanced up at the lush branches above me. "Not reading, but watching them and doing homework. I don't think I could focus with as loud as those things are."

"You get used to it."

"Mina, you ready?" Alec shouted to me.

"Yeah, just a sec." I took another sip of my water and then set it in the grass before standing. "Why don't you ride with Shane?" I asked Becca as I brushed off my bottom.

"Nah, I'll let him go a couple laps without me first. Let his temper cool off."

"All right, but I am getting you out there today. Mark my words." I pointed my index finger at her and narrowed my eyes.

"Okay." She laughed.

I jogged over to where Alec was waiting.

"You and Becca seem to be hitting it off well," Alec said as I climbed on the four-wheeler behind him. "Told you she was pretty cool."

"Yeah, she's nice. Wish I could say the same about her boyfriend."

"Shane is a good guy. He's different. He has one of those personalities you either love or hate."

Right now, as things stood between us, I was leaning toward hate. I didn't say so, though. Instead, I wrapped my arms around Alec's waist.

"Better hold on tighter than that," he insisted.

"Why? You plan on giving me the ride of a lifetime?"

"You bet."

As soon as I adjusted my grip, he took off. Dust flew behind us as wind whipped against my face and arms. I glanced around Alec, trying to see where the others were in relation to us. Shane was in the lead with Benji trailing close behind him. We barreled around the first corner, closing in on the guys, and laughter bubbled up my throat. My grip around Alec's waist tightened, and I pressed my chest flush against his back, making sure I wouldn't fall off as we drifted around the next corner.

"Told you you'd better hold on tighter," he shouted over the roar of his four-wheeler.

"Can this thing go any faster?" I asked even though I wasn't unimpressed with its speed.

"Faster, she says?" Alec chuckled as he twisted the throttle until it wouldn't go anymore.

The wind stung my face, causing my eyes to water. Trees blurred by and the sun beat down on my shoulders, but I didn't mind. I was having fun. Never had I felt such a rush of adrenaline through my system. How had Becca not enjoyed this? How could she sit out each time the guys brought their four-wheelers to the track?

I lost count of how many times we went around, but when I noticed Shane stopping at the bed of his truck, I tapped on Alec's shoulder, letting him know I wanted to take a break too. He slowed immediately.

"You done?"

"No, I just need a sip of water."

"Yeah, I could use something, too." He pulled up beside Shane and waited for me to slip off the back of his four-wheeler before he did. "So, what do you think? Is it as fun as you thought it would be?"

"Better." I started to where I'd left my water. Becca scooped it up and held it out to me. It was nearly warm from the heat. "You ready to ride with Shane once or twice?" I asked her.

"Yeah, I guess." She chewed her bottom lip. Why was she being so mousy about it? Did Shane not like her riding with him? Was he so selfish he didn't want to share his four-wheeler with anyone? Was she nervous about riding?

"Let's go, then." I motioned for her to get up, then twisted the cap off my water and took a swig. "Becca is riding with Shane this time. We should have a race," I said as I wiggled my brows at Alec.

"Really?" Alec shifted his gaze from me to Becca. "Out of all the times we've come here, I've seen you ride like twice."

Becca said something, but I wasn't paying attention. I was too busy having a showdown with Shane. The second I mentioned Becca was riding with him, his gaze had drifted to me, and I could tell he wasn't happy about the change I'd persuaded in her. What was his deal?

"Is that okay with you?" Becca asked as she stepped between Shane and me, blocking my view of him uninten-tionally.

"What?" he asked. His tone was rough and harsh. It had Becca's body tensing instantly.

"If I ride with you a couple of laps. Is that okay?"

"Yeah, I guess. I just don't see why the sudden change of heart. You've always been fine sitting in the shade, watching."

Becca shrugged. "I don't know. I just think it might be fun today."

"Fine, whatever. Hop on."

I took another sip of my water and watched as she climbed onto the back of Shane's four-wheeler. She looked so tiny and frail, but I could make out the buzz of excitement vibrating from her. Shane said something as she wrapped her arms around his waist, but over the sound of Benji revving his engine as he passed by I couldn't make out what.

"Ready for another round?" Alec asked as he slipped back onto his four-wheeler.

"Oh yeah."

I positioned myself behind him again and wrapped my arms around his waist. This time I knew to hold on tighter than I had before. I didn't mind. In fact, I relished the feel of his abs beneath my fingertips.

When Alec took off this time, I was prepared. We raced around the track a couple of times, passing Benji and gaining on Shane and Becca. She molded against Shane's back while she gazed over his shoulder. A wide smile had plastered itself on her face that had my grin growing. Mainly because I liked to think I was the reason for it. After all, I'd talked her into riding.

Shane sped up, putting more distance between us once he noticed we were neck and neck with him. Becca glanced at me and laughed. Yeah, it was safe to say she was enjoying herself. I tightened my grip on Alec's waist as he picked up speed, trying to catch up to them, and a laugh burst from my chest.

It was safe to say I was enjoying myself as well, more than I'd thought I would, considering some of my company.

7

An hour later, we all sat around drinking more water and eating the chips and sandwiches Becca had thought to bring. I wasn't a big fan of the bread she'd used—sourdough wasn't my favorite—but I was so hungry I didn't care. It was nearly three thirty in the afternoon, and I hadn't eaten lunch.

"Think I can take that for a spin around the track by myself?" I asked, nodding toward Alec's four-wheeler. He'd parked it beside Shane and Benji's in a shaded area so the seats and handles wouldn't get hot while we took a food break.

Alec paused mid-chew. "You serious?"

"Why wouldn't I be?"

"Okay."

"Okay? You're just going to let her ride by herself?" Shane asked as though it was the most absurd thing he'd ever heard.

"Yeah." Alec shrugged. "Why not?"

"Uh, because she's never driven one before."

"Gotta start somewhere," Alec insisted.

"Whatever, man. I just don't think it's a good idea."

"Nobody asked you," I said, unable to contain myself. I didn't like Shane. The more I was around him, the more I realized this.

"Kind of like no one asked if I was okay with you being here," he snapped.

"Whoa," Alec said. He held a hand out to Shane as though to stop him from saying anything more. "That wasn't cool. Why should I ask you if she could come? This is my uncle's property, or have you forgotten? I don't know what your problem is, but I think you need to chill."

I hated my presence causing such a rift between Alec and his friend, but I couldn't deny I enjoyed hearing him defend me yet again.

"Seriously, man," Benji agreed as he crammed another wad of dip in his mouth now that he was finished eating. "Tone it down."

Shane shook his head and dropped his gaze to his sandwich. He crammed the remainder of it into his mouth and chewed with an intense level of force.

The entire atmosphere of the place had changed. Tension hung heavily in the air. I polished off the rest of my chips and headed toward Alec's four-wheeler. He was quick to follow.

"Sorry about him. I'm not sure what his deal is today," Alec said as I situated myself behind the handlebars. It felt awkward. Maybe it was because I was so short. I had to sit straight and lean forward in order to reach the handles.

"It's okay. Totally not your fault your friend is super moody for a guy."

Alec laughed. "He is a super moody, isn't he?"

"Only when it involves me or his girlfriend. Maybe he has a thing against girls." It wasn't that and I knew it. Shane just didn't enjoy being around a girl who had a little backbone. He wanted his girlfriend to be placid and sit there, watching while he had all the fun.

I hated guys like him.

"I don't know," Alec said as he scratched the back of his neck. The conversation was making him nervous. I could sense it. We needed a topic change.

"So, Teach, how do I start this bad boy up?"

Alec seemed to relax. He flipped into teacher mode and told me the important things, like how to turn it on and where the gas and brake were. It was a short lesson, because really, what was there to know after being told where the gas and brake were?

"Think you've got it?"

I nodded. "Yeah, totally."

A wide grin spread onto my face as I reached for the key and cranked the engine to life.

"Remember, don't just gas it. Start nice and slow," Alec reminded me.

I gave it a little gas. The engine revved and propelled me forward a few inches.

"Good, go easy. Once you get on the track you can give it some gas and really let it rip."

"Got it," I said as I eased on the gas. My sweaty hand slipped and I jerked forward, barely missing Alec's foot. He jumped back in the nick of time. My hands flew off the handles and came to my mouth. "I'm so sorry!"

"I'd watch out if I were you. Might lose a foot over there." Benji chuckled from where he sat with Becca and Shane.

"Yeah, yeah," Alec said as he waved away Benji's words. A lopsided grin formed on his face. One I found so adorable I wanted to kiss him. He took a couple steps back, giving me some space. "Go ahead. Give it hell."

I made sure to give it a little gas so I could ease away from him. Once all four tires were on the dirt track, and I'd lined myself up properly, I gave it more gas. The wind whipped against my face as I made my way around the first corner. By the time I reached the long stretch of little hills, I was more comfortable on the beast of a thing. Laughter bellowed from somewhere deep inside my chest. I'd ridden go-carts before, but they were nothing compared to this. I could clearly see why the guys came out here most weekends to tear up the track.

After my third round, Benji joined me on the track. I gave the four-wheeler more gas so I could pass him. Seconds later, he flew around me faster than I thought four-wheelers could go. He tipped his head back and let out a "Yee-haw!" It sounded muffled. I wasn't sure if it was because of the loud engines of the four-wheelers or the extra-large dip he'd crammed into his mouth. I went around the track once more before coming in slowly beside where Alec stood. His arms were folded across his chest as he watched me.

"How did I do?" I asked.

"Perfect." He grinned. "You looked like a natural out there."

"I felt like a natural." It was the truth. The wind against

my face. The sunshine beaming down on me. The raw power with the flick of a wrist. I'd already added riding a motorcycle to my bucket list next, because it had to be even more exhilarating than this.

"Can I hop on?" Alec asked.

My gaze drifted to where Shane and Becca were still sitting. Tension radiated between them, and it looked as though they were in deep conversation. He was probably complaining to her about me.

"How about I take Becca for a ride first?" The words slipped out of my mouth without much thought behind them. Becca glanced at me at the mention of her name, and her wide doe-like eyes brightened. I couldn't be sure if she wanted to ride, or if she was looking for a way out of whatever conversation she'd been locked in with Shane.

"Sure, yeah. Go ahead." Alec smirked. "I'm loving all this confidence you've gained in a matter of minutes on the thing. Sort of wish I'd thought to bring you out here sooner."

"Me too. I love it," I said. I noticed Becca stand. She dusted her bottom off before starting toward me. Shane grabbed her wrist. He said something to her, but I couldn't hear what. It didn't look like he was too happy about Becca agreeing to ride with me. "Becca, you coming?" I asked.

She freed herself from Shane's grip. "Yeah."

Shane watched the two of us as I popped the four-wheeler in reverse and backed onto the track. I didn't look at him, but I could feel his gaze on me.

"Everything okay between you two?" I asked Becca once we were facing the opposite direction from the guys.

"Yeah, he's just upset. Like I said before, he thinks I'm making him look like an ass today," Becca said as she adjusted her arms around my waist. I could tell there was something more to it, but she didn't want to tell me.

"You're not making him look like an ass; he's making himself look like one," I said.

"I know, but it would take a miracle to get him to realize that," Becca said. "He's not really bothering me, though. This is the most fun I've had out here in a long time. Thanks for getting me to ride one of these things again."

"Don't worry. The fun is just getting started."

I gave Alec's four-wheeler more gas, and we drove around the track twice before deciding to head back to Alec. I didn't want to keep him waiting any longer for a ride. Becca had seemed to have fun. I'd heard her laughing a few times when Benji caught up to us and made strange faces. That guy was a trip.

"Done already? It looked like you two were having fun," Alec insisted when I came to a rolling stop in front of him.

Becca hopped off from behind me, but she didn't rush to where Shane was. She went to the cooler and pulled out another bottle of water instead.

"We were." My lips twisted into what I hoped looked like an innocent smile. "And I would like to go around a couple more times, but this time with Becca on her own four-wheeler. Think you guys can let the girls have the track for a little while?"

"Oh, I don't know," Becca said. She shook her head as she placed the cap back on her water.

"Come on, it'll be fun."

Benji came to a rolling stop beside where Becca stood. He reached into the cooler and pulled out a bottle of water.

"No. There's no way I'm letting Becca drive my four-wheeler," Shane snapped.

"Why not?" I swore if he said something about female drivers not being good, I was going to hop off this thing and deck him.

"I've never seen her drive one in her life," Shane insisted.

"You've never seen me drive one either. I managed to do okay," I said as I glance at Alec for affirmation. "Right?"

"Yeah, you did great." He smiled.

"Jesus, dude," Benji said. He flicked the dip from his mouth onto the ground before cracking open his bottle of water and placing it to his lips. "Don't get your panties all in a wad. Becca can drive mine."

I knew I liked Benji.

"Awesome." I switched Alec's four-wheeler into reverse. "Go ahead, Becca. Climb on. Let's go around once or twice, and then we'll let the guys have the track again." I didn't want Alec thinking I was hogging his four-wheeler.

"You sure?" Becca asked Benji as he slipped off and motioned for her to get on.

"Go for it." He took another swig of his water. "You know how to work everything, right?"

"Gas, brake, reverse," Becca said, pointing to each.

"What are you waitin' for, then?"

Becca switched the four-wheeler into reverse and eased her way backward. Before she changed gears, I caught her gaze drift to Shane. His face looked red, and I didn't think it was from the heat. Had Becca wanting to enjoy herself out here today ruined his day that badly? How could he be ticked off at that? I didn't get him.

"We're going to do a lap or two. Okay?" I asked Alec.

"Sure," he said. "I'm going to see if we have any more chips."

"One step ahead of you, brother," Benji said as he tossed a bag to Alec. The two of them walked to the shaded area where Shane was sitting.

Becca and I flew around the track being sure to give each other ample room. When we decided to give the guys back their four-wheelers, my hands were tingling and my fingers were stiff. My grip must have been too tight. It was worth it, though. I'd never had so much fun before.

Alec pecked me on the lips after I slipped off his four-wheeler. The kiss surprised me. He hadn't shown much public affection toward me today. I felt like it was a big deal. My insides reflected this as butterflies flew through my stomach.

"Did you have fun?" he asked. His eye appraised me in a way that had my heart thumping hard.

"Oh yeah." I made my way to where Becca was sitting beneath the shady tree, feeling Alec watching me walk, wondering if Shane had said anything to her. If he had, it hadn't been more than a few words. Maybe that was a good thing.

"Hey, um, where do you use the restroom? I really have to pee," I muttered when I reached her.

She hitched her thumb over her left shoulder. "To the woods."

"Thanks," I grumbled as I started toward the woods. Popping a squat was never fun. Guys had it is so dang easy.

I made my way through the thick foliage and slipped behind a big tree. Pulling down my jeans and panties, I popped a squat like my mom had taught me when I was little.

My gaze drifted around the woods. Something dark red and crusty a few feet away captured my attention. After I drip dried and pulled my panties and jeans up, I headed over for a closer look. Was it blood? Deep scratches marred the ground in places, too. The closer I looked, the odder the scene seemed. There was blood speckled along some of the foliage. Had a struggle happened here?

Friday night.

The memory of the wolf I'd heard boomed through my mind. He'd sounded injured in his final howl. Was this from him? I thought for a moment. Was there anyone in the pack who'd recently been hurt? I couldn't think of anyone. They would have come to Gran for one of her remedies if so. Maybe someone had taken an animal down. I glanced around, checking out the surrounding area.

There was nothing.

No carcass. Nothing. Wolves didn't take down many animals—it wasn't necessary for our survival like depicted in books and on TV—but when we did, something was always left behind.

What had happened here, then?

"You okay?" Becca asked from somewhere close. I hadn't noticed she'd followed me into the woods.

"Yeah, I'm fine. Just found a little blood on the ground. At least I think that's what it is," I said even though I knew.

Becca stepped to where I was. Her nose wrinkled when she spotted the area in question. "That's definitely blood. Someone must've been hunting."

"I didn't think anything was in season, though."

"That's never stopped some of the guys around here. Especially not Shane and his brothers."

This didn't surprise me. I didn't think Shane would be one to follow rules. Since the apple rarely fell too far from the tree, I imagined his entire family was the same.

My stomach knotted as a thought occurred to me.

"Do Shane and his family hunt here on Alec's uncle's property?"

"Year round even though Alec has asked them not to," Becca said, causing my heart to beat faster. "Actually, I think him and his brothers were out here the other night."

We started walking back toward the shaded area beside the track.

"How many brothers does he have?"

"He's the youngest of three. His oldest brother is like twenty-eight and the other one is twenty-six."

"Wow, that's a big age gap between them and Shane."

"I think that's part of why he's such a jerk most of the time. He's attention hungry. Even though he's not an only child, he sure does act like one." She rolled her eyes.

"Does he get along with his brothers?" I wasn't sure why I'd asked. What I really wanted to know was if Shane or his brothers had ever mentioned seeing wolves out here. Like maybe on Friday night?

"Oh yeah. Well, most of the time. It's a weird relationship really. Shane is always feeling like he has to prove himself to his brothers. He strives too hard sometimes to make them proud of him. I think it's because they were his father figures growing up. His dad died when Shane was a kid. Hunting accident. People said it was a bear mauling."

"That's awful."

"Yeah. His mom was devastated. She still has lapses of depression from it all."

We situated ourselves beneath the shady tree again. The boys were still racing around the track, oblivious to us.

"So, what do Shane and his brothers hunt out here?" I asked because I wanted to know more.

"Deer, wild turkeys, sometimes squirrels."

"Is that all that's out here?"

"Why?" Suspicion sifted through her eyes. My guard went up.

"I've never paid much attention I guess. I mean, are there still bears here?" It was the scariest, largest creature we'd mentioned in our conversation. I hoped it would be enough to curb her suspicion.

"I'm sure there are, but I haven't seen any. I have seen wolves, though."

I forced my face into a neutral expression and tried to play it cool as she watched me too closely. "Really? I've never seen any."

"Yeah, well, these woods really aren't that safe at night," Becca said. Her words were stern. It wasn't as though she was warning me about the wolves, but about something else. Her boyfriend, perhaps? Did Becca know more than she was letting on? A shiver slipped along my spine. I'd never been around a human who knew my kind existed. "But, you probably already knew that."

I blinked and then opened my mouth to say something, but Alec cruised to a stop a few feet in front of us. He let the engine of his four-wheeler idle.

"I think we're done for the day," he yelled over the engine "It's a little after five. I'm pretty sure I'm going to be sunburned all to hell, and this heat is starting to get to me." It was the first time I'd noticed how pink his skin was.

"Man, it is hot out," Benji shouted as he eased his four-wheeler onto Alec's trailer. He wiped at his forehead with the edge of his T-shirt. "I'm gonna need to drink a gallon of my momma's lemonade."

"You're always talking about her lemonade. It's not like it's homemade or anything. It's freaking Crystal Light," Alec teased.

"Is too homemade. She makes it at home, don't she?" Benji grinned like an idiot.

I laughed. I couldn't help it.

"I should get going too," Shane insisted. "We're supposed to have a family dinner tonight."

"Eating what you killed out here Friday night?" I said, unsure why the words propelled past my lips. I wished I could take them back the instant they'd slipped free.

"Wouldn't you like to know?" Shane narrowed his eyes on me and worked his jaw back and forth. My stomach dropped to my toes.

"How did you know he caught something? Actually, how did you know he'd been hunting out here?" Alec asked. His gaze narrowed on me.

"Um, I went pee behind that tree over there," I said, pointing to it. "There are signs of a struggle—blood on the ground, scratches. I showed it to Becca, and she said Shane and his brothers like to hunt here sometimes. Figured they must've caught something Friday night. Becca said they were here."

"I thought I told you my uncle didn't want you hunting here anymore," Alec said, shifting his full attention to Shane.

"You did, but it wasn't that big of a deal. We caught a couple rabbits; that's it."

Rabbits? Really? There was a heck of a lot more blood and destruction back there than what any rabbit I'd ever seen could do. Unless he'd killed the Easter bunny. I kept my mouth shut, though. It seemed like I'd already said enough.

"I don't care. Neither does my uncle. He told me no one could hunt here anymore. I've been respectful of that. Benji has been respectful of that. Everyone I know has except you." Alec hopped off his four-wheeler and started strapping it in place. His movements were jerky. "It's not safe, and you know it."

My breath caught in my throat. "Why is it not safe?"

I knew why they would *think* it might not be, but did they know the real reason?

Alec stopped what he was doing and directed his gaze toward me. His eyes bored into mine. I got the impression he wanted to tell me something, but wasn't sure how to word it.

"You have to know about these woods. I mean, you live in Mirror Lake Trailer Park. You've lived in Mirror Lake your whole life. You probably know better than anyone what I'm talking about," he said.

Was it me, or was there a certain level of softness hanging in his tone, almost as though he was sorry we were even having this conversation? My heart thundered against my rib cage. Did he think I was a wolf? What about my family?

"The wolves. You've heard about the wolves, right? All the rumors and theories that fly around this town about everyone who lives in the trailer park," Benji said. "Some people in town actually think y'all livin' in the trailer park are werewolves. Freakin' whack jobs," Benji muttered as he strapped his four-wheeler down while shaking his head. It was clear he didn't believe in the rumors.

"My uncle is not a whack job," Alec snapped. I'd never seen him angry before. It was jarring. "He saw what he saw. I believe him."

I licked my lips, unbelieving this conversation. "What did he see?"

"A wolf. It bit him," Alec said. He was dead serious.

I didn't know how I should react. Should I make a joke about his uncle becoming a werewolf now even though I knew it wasn't a possibility? Should I act surprised? Scared?

"Since then, he doesn't want anyone hunting here. Especially not at night or early morning," Alec said.

"Why not during the day? Why does he let you use this piece of property to race your four-wheelers on if he's worried about someone else getting attacked?" It seemed like the only logical question.

"Wolves don't come out during the day. They're night creatures," Shane surprised me by saying. My gaze drifted to him. There was something glistening in his eyes I didn't like. It was almost as though he enjoyed seeing me squirm. Maybe because he knew why?

Wolves didn't hunt like he was insinuating, though. But I couldn't tell them that. It would only make me sound crazy. Or worse, it would put me on Shane and his brother's radar. I had a feeling they weren't your average hunters. They knew werewolves existed, and they knew how to hunt them.

My mind reeled.

Who was missing from the pack? What had Shane and his brothers done with them?

I needed to go home.

Shane's eyes were glued to me as he loaded his four-wheeler onto the trailer. Chill bumps erupted across my skin.

I knew I didn't like the guy, but now I had an even bigger reason.

"Here's your strap," Alec said, tossing one to him. "Tighten it up yourself." He jumped off the trailer and headed straight for the cab of his truck. I picked up the trash near where we'd all been sitting, struggling to force my heart to slow its fast-paced rhythm and the tension to leak from my muscles. I needed to relax, but I couldn't because I could feel Shane's eyes boring into my back.

"Here, you can put that in this," Becca said. She handed me a plastic grocery bag.

"Thanks."

After I was finished picking up trash, I made my way to Alec's truck and climbed in. Benji scooted in beside me.

"Good job out there today. You're one hell of a racer," he said as he flashed me a grin. Tiny pieces of dip were trapped between his bottom front teeth. It was disgusting.

"Thanks," I said before motioning to his mouth. "And you've got a little something going on."

Benji flipped down the visor and glanced in the mirror. He showed his teeth so that he could see what I was talking about. "What? You mean all this sexy shit stuck between my teeth?"

I laughed. "Yeah, that would be it."

Alec chuckled as he cranked the engine of his truck and popped it into drive. "That's disgusting, man."

We all laughed as he pulled away from the track. An uneasy feeling still stirred in the pit of my stomach I couldn't shake, though. I needed to get home. I needed to make sure each of the pack members was accounted for.

8

When I stepped through the front door, the scent of savory spices hit my nose. Gran was cooking, which also meant the trailer was one hundred degrees inside. Even without the oven being used.

"Made it back in one piece I see," Gran said without looking at me as she continued stirring a large pot at the stove. The pork chops sizzled in one of her cast-iron skillets.

"Why wouldn't she?" Dad asked.

He was on the couch. He shifted around, repositioning the heating pad against his lower back and propped his feet up on the coffee table. A glass of water sat near him, which was surprising, considering the time of day. Was it possible he hadn't started drinking yet? I knew my answer without having to think too hard. The closer to a full moon we came, the less pain he was in. Gracie sat beside him, her nose buried in another paranormal book.

The entire scene looked so normal. It was slightly jarring.

"I went four-wheeling today," I said as I started toward

the fridge. My clothes were already sticking to me from my day in the sun, but the heat in here was making it worse. Something to drink was necessary.

"Who did you go four-wheeling with?" Dad asked.

I pulled a cup from the cabinet near the fridge and filled it with tap water. "Alec and some of his friends."

"Was it all boys?" Dad asked with a grumble.

"No, there was another girl," I said as I took a sip from my water and headed to the couch.

I passed the AC unit in the window. Warm air blew out of it instead of cold. It was time for a new one. Who knew when that would happen, though.

"As long as you weren't in the middle of the woods with a group of damn boys," Dad said as he adjusted his heating pad again. His face reddened. He reached for his bottle of painkillers on the table and dumped one or two in his hand.

"Even if it were all boys, it wouldn't matter. I can handle myself," I insisted.

"I know you can handle yourself, but I still worry." He reached for his water and swallowed the pills. "You're my daughter. I'll always worry."

It was the sweetest thing he'd said to me in months. In fact, it had me choking up a little. Moments like these were so few and far between.

"You got home just in time," Gran called from the kitchen, and she pulled plates down from a cabinet. "Dinner is done. We're eating early tonight. Come get it."

She didn't have to tell me twice. This was my favorite meal. Even though I'd eaten a sandwich and bag of chips earlier, I still managed to work up an appetite for Gran's cooking.

Once we were seated at the table, all I could think about was how long it had been since we'd eaten as a family. A meal where Dad hadn't been shit-faced already.

When he stood and headed to the kitchen, I watched him carefully, hoping he was going for the salt or maybe even the pepper. Instead, he swung the fridge door open and grabbed a beer. My heart shrank in on itself as I watched him twist the cap off and take a long swig. He hadn't even given his pills enough time to work before he reached for a damn bottle. Maybe if he had, he wouldn't need to drink so much this close to the full moon.

No one said a word to him when he sat back down, but I knew we were all thinking the same thing.

"Where did you go four-wheeling at?" Gracie asked in an attempt to clear the air and start a conversation.

"Not far from here. Alec's uncle owns a piece of land that butts up against the lake. They created a dirt track there," I said as I stabbed at my black-eyed peas.

Images of the blood I'd seen and the scratch marks on the ground flashed through my mind. I wondered if Gran or my dad knew if anyone had gone missing from our pack or been hurt. Did they know Alec's uncle had been bitten a while back? Did they know who did it?

"Alec? What's his last name again?" Dad asked before I could voice any of my questions.

"Thomas."

His face scrunched up in disapproval. "I'm not too keen on the Thomases."

This surprised me. It was rare he ever said he wasn't too keen on anyone. Generally, he liked everyone he met. Then again, maybe it was because he was a friendly drunk.

"Why not?" I asked around a mouthful of food. Gran glared at me, and I knew it was because she was chastising my table manners, or lack thereof.

"One night when Westley was out for a run he ran into David Thomas. I think he's the uncle you're talking about who owns that piece of land you were on today," Dad said before taking another long swig from his beer. The bottle was nearly empty already. He sure knew how to put them away. "Anyway, Westley was running around the lake, burning off some energy alone one night while that Thomas guy was camping on his property. It was during deer season. I guess he must've thought Westley was a deer or saw his wolf form and got scared. Either way, he shot at Westley. He missed and Westley took off like a bat out of hell, but it didn't stop David from pursuing him. Chased him for miles he said. Shot at him numerous times, too. Until the asshole ran out of bullets, which also happened to be when he had Westley cornered. Westley did the only thing he could—he bit him on the arm to escape. I don't blame him. I would've done a hell of a lot worse if it had been me. I think that Thomas guy got lucky."

Westley, Eli's dad, was who had attacked Alec's uncle?

Eli's dad was our Alpha. There was no way he would do anything to jeopardize our packs safety. I could only imagine how scared he must've felt to push himself to the point of biting a human. Alec had made it sound like his uncle was viciously attacked. I knew there were two sides to every story, but wow.

Was this why everyone didn't like the idea of me dating Alec? I guess I could understand, but still. Alec wasn't his uncle.

"The main point of that story is," Gran said as serious as I'd ever heard her. "He was alone. Never go on a run alone."

All of us nodded in agreement, knowing how much drilling the point into our minds meant to Gran. A decade ago, our grandfather had gone on a run alone. He never came back. A hunter shot him. His body was found at the edge of the woods the next day by a pack member. He was no longer in wolf form, but instead had transformed into his human form. This wasn't uncommon. When injured while in wolf form, a werewolf always transformed into their human state to heal. Even if the wound happened to be fatal.

We cremated my grandpa later that afternoon and held a wake in celebration of his life. I'd been seven.

Since then Gran always stressed to everyone in the pack not to go on runs alone. She always said it was best to run with a buddy or wait until the full moon run and go with the pack.

Running with the pack during the full moon was safest. Not because there was safety in numbers, but because of the deal our pack had struck with the Caraway witches of Mirror Lake decades ago.

"I know," I said as I sliced into a thick piece of pork chop. "But, I might not have to worry about that. My wolf gene might not be triggered."

Gran sighed as though she was sick of hearing me say those words. "You will. You're just a late bloomer. Always have been," Gran insisted.

"How far are we from the next full moon again?" Gracie asked.

"What does it matter to you?" I demanded. She was still a

few years away from having to drink the nasty tea meant to trigger the werewolf gene.

Maybe triggering it was a bad word to use. It didn't just trigger the gene, it created some sort of allergic reaction within the body that awakened the dormant gene inside. At least for most. Sylvie Hess was a different story.

"Maybe that's my entertainment," she snapped and then stuck her tongue out.

I rolled my eyes and opened my mouth to say something smart-ass in response, but Gran spoke before I could.

"Ten days."

"I can't believe it's only ten days away," Dad said as he took the final swig of his beer and stood to retrieve another. His limp was becoming less prominent, but not enough. While it wouldn't disappear once the full moon was upon us, his pain would lessen enough to make his limp barely noticeable when he walked. It was one of the reasons I thought the moon was so magical. "The month seemed to blur by."

I knew why his months blurred by, we all did, but just like before we all kept our mouths shut about it. What was the point? Hashing it out would only drive him to drink more. I'd seen it happen numerous times when Mom was still around.

I shoved another forkful of Gran's black-eyed peas in my mouth to help me stay quiet. They were seasoned to perfection just like always. It was the greens I'd never cared for. Of course, I didn't have the heart to tell her.

"I've got two days until my harvest of salvia is ready," Gran said.

My stomach twisted at the mention of the powerful herb. You'd think after so many times of drinking the tea she made with it, I'd have gotten over the taste by now. Frankly, I didn't think it was possible.

"What's the matter, Mina, not ready for another taste so soon?" Gracie asked. I didn't care for her snotty tone.

"You just wait until you have to start drinking it. Then, we can talk about the taste and whether you're ready each month."

That shut her up. Her time was coming. She'd be forced to drink the same tea on a monthly basis until she became Moon Kissed, or didn't.

"I damn sure don't miss it," Dad said with a shiver. "I never could get used to the horrible taste. Nothing helped, not even plugging my nose. I had to down it as quickly as possible and pray I didn't puke it right back up."

"Exactly! I can't wait till I don't have to drink it anymore." I chuckled. It was nice to hold a conversation with him, even if he'd already started drinking.

"It's not that bad. You two exaggerate things," Gran insisted. "Aren't you girls going to eat your greens? Mina, I thought they were your favorite."

"They are. I'm just full," I said, still unable to bring myself to tell her the truth about them. No matter how much sugar or ham hock she added, they always tasted bitter.

"And why is that? You knew I was cooking."

My stomach flip-flopped. She wasn't happy with me. "I don't know. I think it's the peas. They're filling."

If I told her I'd eaten a late lunch, she'd have my head. Especially since she mentioned what she was making for dinner before I left.

Gran's gaze never wavered from me, but I couldn't bring myself to lift my eyes to hers. The second I did, she would know I was lying. Heck, she probably already knew. Her intuition about things was strong.

"Do you think I can go to the movies tomorrow night?" Gracie asked, saving me from Gran's wrath, even though she didn't realize it.

"Who are you going with?" Dad asked.

"Callie and Violet," Gracie said, naming two girls who lived in the park.

"No boys?" Dad asked.

"No," Gracie said. She'd responded too quickly. I knew she was lying. Gran did, too. Her eyes narrowed on Gracie.

"I don't see why you can't," Dad said. He pulled out his wallet and handed her a twenty. Since when did it cost twenty dollars to go to the movies? "Here, I don't have anything smaller. Bring me back my change."

And there it was. I knew there was no way he was going to give her twenty bucks to see a movie. It would tap into his beer money.

9

When we were finished with dinner, Gracie helped me put up the leftovers and wash the dishes. It was a nighttime ritual in the Ryan household. Gran cooked the meals, and Gracie and I took care of the cleanup. Dad drank.

After I handed Gracie the last plate to dry, I headed to the front door, ready for some fresh air. The trailer was still too hot. Plus, a walk to clear my head seemed like a good idea. Clips of what I'd seen in the woods earlier and the story Dad had told at dinner shifted through my mind.

I trekked around the trailer park, taking notice of who was home and who wasn't. Not that it would help me figure out who might be missing from the pack. There was no way to account for everyone unless they were standing in front of me. People came and went from the park all the time. We all led busy lives.

Maybe there wasn't anyone missing. Maybe the wolf I'd heard Friday night and the blood I found today weren't connected. Maybe Shane and his brothers had bagged a rabbit like he'd claimed.

My gut told me a different story, though.

I should have mentioned something to Gran and Dad about it, but after hearing Dad's story, I hadn't wanted to. What if I told them, and they thought Alec had something to do with it? What if they forbid me from seeing him because of it? I couldn't let that happen.

Alec was a good guy. I cared for him. A lot.

I spotted Eli unloading plywood from the back of his truck when I made my way back toward my trailer. He placed the piece of wood on a makeshift table and began measuring. I paused, watching him mark off a couple notches on the wood in preparation to make a cut. He bit the inside of his cheek and pulled his brows together as he concentrated on what he was doing. I'd never seen him so lost in something before. Then again, I tried to spend as little time around him as possible due to the weird pull I felt toward him.

I continued walking to my place, but couldn't bring myself to look away from him. His gaze lifted to mine. It was as though he could feel my eyes on him.

"Hey, Mina. Care to help me with something?" he asked. The ghost of a smile twisted at his lips. It had me wondering if he actually needed my help, or if he just wanted my company.

"Depends on what it is, I guess," I said.

"Come hold my wood for me," he said as his eyes narrowed playfully.

Electricity zinged through my stomach. "Whatever." I rolled my eyes and continued walking.

"Seriously though, come hold this piece of wood so I can make a clean-cut."

"Isn't that what those clamps are for?" I nodded to the shiny silver clamps hanging off the edge of his makeshift table. While I might not know much about carpentry, I knew enough to recognize what they were for.

"Not at the angle I need it held at."

"Oh." I started toward him, feeling slightly stupid. Maybe he truly did need my help. "What do you want me to do?"

He tapped the edge of the piece of wood. "Put one hand here and the other here."

I stepped closer to do as he said, feeling my stomach summersault at our sudden closeness. "Okay, now what?"

"Now look away. I'd feel horrible if sawdust got in your eyes."

"What about you? Shouldn't you be wearing safety glasses?"

"I'm not worried about me."

I didn't miss the smirk cutting across his face. Warmth splashed through me. I averted my gaze and held on to the wood tightly. "What are you making?"

"I'm replacing the subfloor in front of that leaky window in the dining room," he said as he measured out his notches once more before reaching for the saw. It was something I'd watched my dad do anytime he built something. He'd always said measure twice, cut once. Must be something Eli had heard too. "After this, I need to sand a little more beneath the window and paint the wall. Then, the living room is pretty much done."

"Cool." I was amazed he'd already done so much to the

place. He'd been busy. Which meant he hadn't been working at the bar. "Did you already get fired from the bar?"

"No," he scoffed. "Why would you think that?"

"Because, correct me if I'm wrong, but aren't weekends the busiest time there?"

"Yeah, but Eddie gave me the weekend off since he learned I moved into my own place."

"That was nice."

"Yeah, Eddie's is a pretty cool guy." Eli matched the saw up with the line he'd scratched into the wood. "Hold the piece still. I need to make a straight line."

"Got it." I tightened my grip.

"Look away," he insisted.

A high-pitched buzzing sound spurred from the piece of machinery the second I did. It was horrible, but it was nothing compared to the sharp scent of freshly cut wood wafting to my nose. I hated the smell of sawdust. It tickled my nose worse than pollen.

"Beautiful," Eli said as he admired his work. He swiped sawdust off the plywood. It floated through the air before falling to land on my toes. I knew I should have worn my sneakers before taking a walk around the park. I instantly moved to wipe my feet clean. "Sorry about that. Didn't realize you weren't wearing real shoes."

"These are real shoes," I said.

"Sure they are," he muttered. "Want to come inside and see what I've done to the place so far?"

I hesitated. The last time we'd been together had left me feeling hot and bothered, but I was curious to see what he'd done to the place. Maybe this time would be different. If I kept distance between us, it would be. "Okay, sure."

"I'm not twisting your arm. You don't have to if you don't want to." He snorted.

"I don't have anything better to do."

"Nice to know, I guess." He started up the new steps he'd built since the last time I stopped by and held the door open for me. I slipped past him and inside, careful not to touch him. "Glad I'm at the top of your list of people to visit when you have nothing better to do."

"I didn't mean it like that, I just..." My words caught in my throat as I took in what he'd done to the place the last couple days. While it wasn't finished, he had still accomplished so much in such a short span of time. "Wow, have you taken a second to sleep since the last time I was here?"

Eli crossed to the dining room window. A section of the floor had already been cut out and the rotten piece removed. I watched as he bent down to position the new piece into place. His silver chain dangled in the air, glinting in the sunlight and his arm muscles flexed.

"Of course, but like I said, I've had the weekend off. I wanted to get the easy stuff out of the way."

I wasn't sure what he was deeming easy.

"None of this looks easy." I glanced around, taking it all in. "Well, except for maybe the painting." He'd painted the living room area, and it looked as though he'd started on the dining room when he remembered the leaky window and had to pause.

"Painting might be easy, but it's time-consuming and it sucks," he said before hammering the piece of plywood in place.

"I like painting. I'd rather do that than sand walls and cut plywood or build crap any day."

Painting was therapeutic. I wasn't sure how many times I'd painted mine and Gracie's bedroom, but each time, I felt a sense of energy shift from it. There was no cheaper, or easier, way to change the feel of a room than paint.

"If you like it so much, there's a brush over there. Get to it," Eli said, nodding toward an abandoned brush sitting in a drip pan. "Why don't you cut in the rest of this dining room for me? Since you don't have anything better to do." He winked.

"Will you just drop that? I didn't mean it the way it sounded," I insisted as I walked over to pick up the paint-brush. I dumped more paint in the tray and sloshed my paint-brush around in it.

The color he picked was neutral. A light beige that would go with about anything. While it wasn't a color I would have chosen—I liked gray tones better than browns—I still thought it beat the nicotine yellow the walls had been before.

"I'm kidding. I know you didn't," Eli said. "As soon as I get this section nailed in, I'll sand the window a little more and then you can paint over here too."

"What makes you think I'm hanging around that long?"

"The way your face lit up when I asked you to paint."

Damn. He was observant, if nothing else. "Touché."

"I don't think I've ever seen someone enjoy painting as much as you."

"I don't like painting pictures or anything. Just walls when I want something to refresh a space."

"I know."

"How could you possibly know that about me?" I tried to add a scoff to my words, but it came out sounding wrong.

"I noticed you change the paint of your bedroom walls

nearly every summer." His words were so smooth. He didn't care that he'd just admitted to watching me. "And before you say it, no. I'm not stalking you. I smelled the paint every summer and could hear you jamming your rap music."

I laughed because it was true. Every summer I tossed open our bedroom window, kicked Gracie out, cranked up some music, and painted the entire room a new color. Eli would know this, because he'd always been my next-door neighbor.

I opened my mouth to say something, but caught him walking my way from the corner of my eye. There was something in his hand, but I wasn't sure what it was until he kneeled beside me to place a cell phone on a docking station I hadn't noticed before. At the press of a button, music filled the trailer. It was just loud enough to send the awkwardness of silence away.

"What is it you like so much about painting?" The heat from his body radiated to me. He hadn't stepped away like I'd thought he would. He was still right up on me.

I licked my lips. "I don't know. I guess it allows me to clear my head. It's a mundane task I don't have to think about. I just do it." I glanced at him from over my shoulder, wanting to judge his reaction to my words and gauge how close he was to me.

"Hmm, is that so?" His lips were so close I could feel his warm breath fluttering across my face. If I lifted onto the tips of my toes, his lips would connect with mine. My toes curled and my heart hammered against my chest. Did I want that? Did I want to kiss Eli? His scent saturated the air around me, intoxicating me. "What are you trying to clear your mind of now?"

"What I saw in the woods." The words fell from my mouth as though they'd been waiting on the tip of my tongue to be said the entire time I'd been in his presence.

The area between his brows furrowed as he took a step back, whatever had been building between us shattered. "What do you mean?"

I released the breath I'd been holding and shifted my attention back to painting the wall. "I'm not really sure, to be honest. Friday night I thought I heard someone from the pack howling in the woods when Alec walked me home." Saying his name in Eli's place seemed wrong for some reason. It made my heart hammer faster and my stomach flip-flop. "I think it was someone going on a run by themselves."

"That's not uncommon. No matter what your Gran says, sometimes you just want to go on a run by yourself."

"Do you run by yourself?" I glanced at him. My insides burned with emotions that surprised me.

"Sometimes."

"You shouldn't." I hated sounding like Gran, but I needed to reiterate what she always said. It was important. "You should always run with someone, Eli. More than one wolf if you can. Or just wait until the full moon and run safely with the pack. That would be best."

"Yeah, yeah, I know." He tossed his hands up in surrender, but it was clear from the smirk twisting his lips and the amusement flickering in the bright green of his eyes, he wasn't taking heed to my warning.

"No. You don't know." I set my paintbrush down and shifted my attention to him fully. "Not only did I hear a wolf running alone, but I also found blood in the woods today when I was with Alec on his uncle's property that butts up against the lake. There were signs of a struggle and blood. I think the wolf I heard had an encounter with a hunter."

His features grew serious. I had his attention now. "Are you sure?"

I nodded but didn't speak. Instead, I allowed him to process what I'd said.

"I thought hunting season was over."

"It's supposed to be, but you know as well as I do not everyone in this town follows those rules."

He smoothed a hand over his face. "Yeah, I know, but I haven't seen anyone in the woods lately."

"Then you got lucky. I don't think whoever was in the woods Friday night was so lucky, though." My stomach twisted.

"You think whoever it was in the woods Friday night was shot?"

I nodded. "I think they were taken, too. There wasn't a body. I think Alec's friend Shane and his brothers took whoever it was."

Eli blew out a long breath. "Even if they did, I haven't heard any talk of anyone missing from the pack. If it happened Friday night, someone would have noticed by now. They would have said something to my dad. He would have sent out a search party, something."

"I know, but..."

"I'm not saying what you think happened didn't. I just think we would have heard something about it by now if it did. I'll keep an ear out, though."

Maybe that was all we could do. I mean, Eli was right. If someone were missing from the pack, we would know it by now. Wouldn't we?

"Okay." I picked up my paintbrush and swirled it through more paint. "I already walked around the trailer park, trying to see if I could spot anyone missing from the pack tonight. It was stupid, but I felt like I had to do something."

"Did you tell your Gran?"

"No. I don't think she'd believe me. I'm actually kind of surprised you did."

"Why wouldn't I believe you?"

"I don't know." I shrugged.

Eli reached for me. His hand came to rest on my forearm and sparks of electricity burst beneath my skin like tiny fireworks at the contact. "You can always come to me about anything, Mina. I'll always believe you."

Warmth filled me, causing my heart to contract and expand so quickly it was a miracle I was still alive. "Thanks."

"You're welcome," he said as he removed his touch. "And you don't have to finish painting that wall if you don't want to. I don't want to keep you."

He did, though. I could sense he wanted me to stay. The crazy part was that I wanted to stay, too.

"Like I said, I don't have anything better to do." I flashed him a small smile and went back to painting.

10

Gravel crunched beneath my feet as I walked from my trailer to Felicia Warren's. I'd agreed to babysit her twins today while she worked an extra shift at Mirror Lake Diner off Main Street. She'd offered to pay me forty bucks, which equaled twenty per kid. It was forty dollars more than I currently had, and the kids weren't bad. They were barely one, which meant they were at a fun stage. Not entirely dependent on someone for everything and easily amused.

I knocked on Felicia's front door and waited. The sounds of someone racing around inside met my ears. She must be late getting ready, as usual. Felicia was always rushing around. I guessed with two babies on your hands time could easily get away from you.

"Come on in," Felicia shouted.

I gripped the knob and twisted, but it didn't budge. I wrapped my knuckles against the door again. "Hey, Felicia. It's locked."

"Hold on," she yelled. Footsteps heading to the door sounded from inside. "Ouch, damn it!" She swung the door open and leaned against its frame, cussing like a sailor under her breath while gripping the bottom of her foot.

"You okay?"

"No. Those damn wooden blocks will be the death of me," she muttered, massaging the bottom of her foot. "Come on in."

I stepped into the single-wide trailer while trying hard not to laugh. The scent of apples and cinnamon floated to my nose. Her place always smelled so good.

"Thanks for doing this for me on such short notice," Felicia said as she hobbled toward the dining room table. She swiped a few strands of honey brown hair away from her eyes and tucked them behind her ear. "I really need the extra money this month."

"No problem. I'm glad I can help." I crammed my hands into the back pockets of my shorts.

Felicia was a single mom. Roughly two summers ago, a rogue wolf came through town and the two of them hit it off. The guy ended up staying with her for months. Everyone in the trailer park thought we'd gained a new member to the pack, but the second Felicia found out she was pregnant, the jerk left town. His name had been Frank, but Felicia liked to call him fucker.

I didn't blame her.

"My shift ends at four, but I'm working a double so my mom will be by after she gets off work to pick up the twins," Felicia said as she tied her apron around her tiny waist.

"What time does your mom get off?"

"Four thirty. She should be here before five. The twins

have been fed and their diapers changed. They didn't sleep worth a shit last night, so they'll probably nap throughout the day for you. Please try not to let them sleep too much. I'd love to get four hours of consecutive sleep tonight for once."

"Got it."

She scooped up her purse and keys off the dining room table and rushed to the living room where the munchkins were snuggled together on an oversized beanbag, watching some cartoon where the characters looked like they were half-fish half-people.

"Bye, sweethearts. Mommy will see you later. Be good for Miss Mina." She kissed both of them on the forehead before dashing to the door. "Thanks again! Call me if you need anything."

"I will. Bye. Have a good day at the diner."

I sat on the couch and proceeded to watch the tail end of whatever cartoon it was the twins were watching. It was actually entertaining. There were some catchy songs. The twins were content to watch it until the end. I even noticed them dancing in their seats a time or two, which had me cracking up.

When the next show came on, they began to show signs of boredom. Farah started kicking Fletcher, which made him cry. I scooped him up and tried to get her to tell him she was sorry or at least show him some affection. She ignored me. When I couldn't get Fletcher to stop crying, I resorted to sitting on the floor with them and trying to play with the blocks Felicia had stepped on. This captured their attention for ten minutes, tops.

They were restless today.

I checked my cell for the time. It was a little after ten. I decided to strap them into their double-seated stroller and go for a walk around the trailer park. The last time I babysat, it was spring and still chilly out. The twins had loved it, though. In fact, they'd been asleep within the first ten minutes. I'd walked around the entire park six or seven times before deciding to risk moving them from the stroller inside. The second I did, they'd woken up and all hell had broken loose.

I wouldn't make the same mistake twice. If they fell asleep during our walk, they were staying where they were until they woke. The temperature was warmer, which meant I could park in the shade and let them sleep.

After situating the twins in their stroller, I flipped the brakes off and started pushing them over the bumpy gravel. Thank goodness the stroller had gigantic jogging meals. While it was a bit of a bumpy ride, the twins didn't seem to mind. In fact, Farah thought it was the funniest thing ever to be jostled around inside the stroller. Fletcher was the fussy one today. All he seemed to want to do was cry.

The trailer park was quiet at ten in the morning. Everyone was either off at work, sleeping still, or puttering around their trailers. Part of me wished I was still sleeping, but I needed the extra money. Gas wasn't going to magically appear in my car anytime soon.

I waved to the Bell sisters as I cruised past their place, hoping to seem as though I was in a hurry. If I stopped, they would talk my ear off. Especially since I had the twins with me. There was no doubt the sisters would pinch their chubby little cheeks until they were nearly bleeding.

"Good morning, Mina," the oldest of the Bell sisters said. I struggled with whether I should make eye contact, knowing once I did it would be all over. In the end, I gave in and glanced at her. Gran would have my head if she found out I'd been rude to one of the sisters.

"Good morning, Ms. Bell," I said as I slowed enough to flash her a polite smile.

"Who have you got there?" the youngest of the Bell sisters asked, craning her neck to see inside the stroller. "Is that the little Warren twins?"

"Yeah, I'm babysitting them today. They're feeling fussy, so I should probably continue with the walk. I think the fresh air is doing them good."

"Fresh air does everyone good, dear," the oldest Bell sister said. Her name was Sable and the youngest was named Selene, but I honestly couldn't remember who was who half the time. They looked so much alike. No one ever called them by their first names anyway. They'd always been known as the Bell sisters and nothing more.

"That it does." I gripped the handle of the stroller tighter and pressed forward. I held my breath, waiting for one of them to call me back but neither did. By some small stroke of luck, I'd been spared this morning.

Thank goodness for small miracles.

When I rounded the corner of Gran's trailer, I felt my muscles relax. The front door was open, but I couldn't hear the TV or smell any food cooking. I continued around the side of it, taking myself out of the Bell sisters' view.

Gran was digging in her garden. It wasn't the largest garden, but it worked. She didn't seem to mind it was long and narrow. She just enjoyed having her own slice of land to grow on. All the herbs for her tinctures, teas, and the bulk of the vegetables we ate grew there. The garden like a second home to Gran. When she wasn't inside cooking, sitting in her recliner reading, or knitting, she could be found out here, soaking up the sun rays and humming a soft melody as she worked with her hands in the dirt.

As much as I wished I enjoyed gardening as much as she did, it wasn't my cup of tea. I liked spending time in nature, but gardening was too much work. I preferred hiking or swimming in the lake. Being bent over while I picked weeds and checked plant leaves for funky spots and bugs wasn't my idea of fun. It was more Gracie's thing than mine. She loved learning about Gran's plants and helping her weed the garden.

Speaking of. Where was Gracie?

She was supposed to help Gran today. When I left this morning, she was up and about, so I wasn't sure where she was.

"Hey, Gran," I said as I pushed the twin's stroller to where she was working. "How's everything looking?" I knew she'd been worried about her lemon balm plants. Gran lived on that herb. She swore there were bugs eating it last week. Also, she'd been worried about the salvia, considering it was almost time to be harvested for the full moon again.

"Better than I expected." She glanced up from the weeds she'd been pulling, her blue eyes glistening with love for her garden.

"That's good," I said, looking around for Gracie. "Where's Gracie? I thought she was supposed to help you today." I hated seeing Gran working out here by herself. Even though I knew she enjoyed being in her garden, it seemed like too much work for a seventy-year-old woman to do alone.

"She's grabbing my pruning shears from inside. I forgot them." Gran smiled at the twins. "Well, hello there, little ones. They are just precious. How have they been for you so far? I see you've already resorted to taking them for a walk."

Gran knew my babysitting secrets because they all came from her. She was a miracle worker when it came to getting kids to behave, or at least be manageable.

She pulled off her gardening gloves and exited the chicken wire gate surrounding her garden.

"They're okay. Fletcher is a little whiny this morning. He's been crying on and off since his mom left for work. She said they didn't get much sleep last night. I hoped taking them for a walk would calm them enough to take a nap so they would be better for me later today. No luck yet, though."

"Fletcher looks like he's seconds from passing out. I can tell by his eyes. Farah, on the other hand, seems wide-awake. If all else fails, at least you'll have a little one-on-one time," Gran said as she touched Farah's hair.

"I'll keep walking and see what happens."

"Let me give you something to give Felicia. It should help the twins sleep better at night for her." Gran motioned for me to follow her around the trailer.

She was always concocting homemade remedies for things. It was actually how she made extra money. She had in-depth knowledge of herbs that everyone in the pack came to her for. Honestly, she fascinated me with it all. Sadly, I was never able to retain anything when she attempted to share it with me. Gracie was different. She took after Gran and soaked in the knowledge.

As we stepped around the trailer, I spotted Gracie talking with Cooper Vargas. They looked chummy from the smile stretched across both their faces. When had she started talking to him? As soon as she spotted Gran and me, she told

Cooper she had to go. She kissed him on the check before heading in our direction. Were Cooper and Gracie an item? When had that happened?

My stomach twisted as knots the size of my fist built while I watched Gracie walk. Her cheeks were tinted pink, and there was a dreamy smile on her face.

Why hadn't she mentioned anything about Cooper to me? We talked about everything. Normally. Lately, though, there hadn't been too much dialog going on between us. It was my fault. Over the last few weeks, I'd been preoccupied with the coming full moon and other things.

"Sorry, Gran. I meant to bring these to you, but Cooper had me sidetracked for a second," Gracie said. Her gaze shifted to me as she passed Gran the shears. It didn't linger on me for long before it dipped it to the twins. "Aw, they've gotten so big!"

"Yeah, they have," I said, trying not to feel upset she hadn't said anything to me about Cooper and her being together.

Gran took the shears from her and headed inside. I debated on how to broach the topic of Cooper with Gracie, but I didn't have time to start anything. Gran came back with a brown glass bottle before I could say anything. She held it out to me and I took it. The label said lavender spray.

"Have Felicia spray the twins bedding before she puts them down for the night. The lavender should help them sleep peacefully for a few hours, if not the entire night. She doesn't need to douse the sheets with it, just a light misting will do," Gran said.

"Okay." The bottle was cool in the palm of my hand, and

I could faintly smell the soothing scent of lavender wafting from it. "Felicia will be happy if it works, I'm sure."

"Oh, it will work. Trust me." Gran winked.

I felt bad for having sounded as though I doubted her. Everything Gran did worked.

"All right, thanks for this. I should probably let you get back to the garden," I said as I pushed the stroller forward, grinding over a larger chunk of gravel.

"If they get to be too much, text me and I'll come help," Gracie said.

"Thanks, but I think I'll manage." My words sounded harsher than I'd intended. Gracie didn't seem to notice, though.

I continued around the neighborhood, only pausing when I came to Taryn's tiny silver bullet of a trailer. It wasn't like the other trailers in the park. Not a single wide. Not a double wide. Instead, one you hitched to the back of a truck and pulled along behind you. It was what I called a gypsy trailer. Ready and waiting for the word to pick up and leave. Not that it ever went anywhere. Taryn was fine living in Mirror Lake Trailer Park with the rest of us. At least I thought she was. Right now, she looked as though she might prefer to be anywhere besides here.

Mascara had smeared down her cheeks and her bottle blond hair was a matted mess. Her nose reddened as she wiped it on the back of her hand. I could see the snot glistening in the sunlight. I'd never seen her like this. Generally, she was somewhat put together and happy.

Something was wrong, and even though I didn't want to admit it, a part of me thought I might know what that something was.

11

"He wouldn't do that. It's what they said down at the station too, but I know him. He wouldn't do that," Taryn said into her phone. She pulled a cigarette out of her pack with shaky fingers and reached for her lighter. I watched as she flicked it with her thumb to no avail. "Damn it, I've already told you! He's gone! Something happened to him!"

I slowed my walk so I could listen to her conversation. The knots in my stomach doubled in size. Was her boyfriend, Glenn, the wolf I'd heard in the woods last Friday night? Was the blood I'd seen his?

Taryn thought something had happened to him. While I wasn't one hundred percent sure the two situations were related, I had a gut feeling they might be.

"Yeah well, my gut is telling me something is wrong, Candace. Aren't you the one who's always telling me to listen to my intuition? Pretty damn ironic that now I am and you're telling me I'm wrong, that I'm overreacting. Screw you," Taryn grumbled before she hung up.

Candace was her older sister. She'd practically raised her when their mother committed suicide after finding out what their father and they were. Apparently, some people could handle the supernatural world better than others could. Candace and Taryn's mother hadn't been one of them. Their dad died shortly after. Everyone said it was from a broken heart. I believed it. I'd seen the effects of one firsthand. Some days I was surprised Dad was still alive.

"Hey, Taryn," I said when she didn't seem to notice me. She flinched at the sound of my voice. "Um...Are you okay?"

"No." She shook her head and took a long drag off her cigarette. "I'm so far from okay it's not even funny."

When she shifted her full attention to me, I could see how distraught she was. Taryn was only two years older than I was, but as I stared at her, it seemed as though she had a decade on me. Her eyes were hollowed out and her body looked frail and bony. She reminded me of a junkie. One an officer would show pictures to teens of to help stop them from doing drugs. It was sad really, because I could remember a time when she was beautiful. Her hair hadn't always been banana yellow from bad box dye jobs, and her face wasn't always so worn with worry.

Life had aged Taryn, and as she sat in a crappy fold-up chair, puffing away on her cigarette, I knew it wasn't done yet.

Especially not if what I thought might have happened to Glenn was true.

"Anything I can do to help?" I asked, even though I knew there was probably nothing.

"Not unless you've seen Glenn." Her dark brown eyes lifted to lock with mine.

"Sorry. I haven't seen him. What happened? Did you two get in a fight?"

I prayed she would tell me that was all it was, the two of them had gotten into an argument and he'd taken off like I knew he'd done in the past. I prayed she'd tell me the last time she saw him was last night.

From the disheveled state she was in, I knew my prayers wouldn't be answered.

"We did," she muttered. Fat tears trickled down her cheeks, and she covered her mouth with her other hand, trying to keep her sobs to a minimum. "The last thing I said to him was to *go to hell*."

"I'm sure he knows you didn't mean it." I pushed the stroller to where she was sitting and popped the brakes on just in case the twins became wiggly, and then I situated myself in the foldout chair beside her. My butt nearly fell through the woven slats making up the bottom. One or more of them were broken. "When did you guys fight? Last night?"

She shook her head as another sob wracked her body. It was another minute or two before she could speak. "No, Friday night. He's been gone since Friday night."

My heart dropped to my stomach, and icy tingles spread outward from my chest. Glenn had been the wolf in the woods. That meant the blood I'd found was most likely his, too.

"We were arguing over something stupid. We'd both been drinking, which made it escalate quicker than it normally would. I said a few things I shouldn't. He started to leave because of it, and I took his truck keys." She pulled in a deep breath and put out her cigarette on the concrete slab we were sitting on. I glanced at Glenn's truck. That was the only reason I thought he was still here. "He shifted and bolted for the damn woods as soon as he saw me pocket his keys. I should've gone after him, but I was so ticked off I couldn't stand to be around him for another second. When he didn't come home Friday night, I thought it was for the best. I thought we both needed some time apart. Time to cool off. When he didn't come home Saturday night either, I started to get a worried. When Sunday came around and there was still no sign of him, I went down to the police station to file a missing person report after trying everyone I could think of who might have seen him and not having any luck."

"What did the police say?"

"Nothing," she scoffed. "Maybe I shouldn't have told them we'd been arguing the night he left. If I'd left that part out, they might have taken the situation more serious. All they told me was that he'd come back once he'd cooled off enough."

"Maybe he will," I said, hoping to refresh any hope she might have had when they'd said it.

"I don't know, Mina. I really feel like something horrible happened to him. I know y'all think we fight all the time, and I'm not going to lie and say we don't, but this isn't like him. Glenn wouldn't leave like this and not come back. If anything, he would've at least come back for his truck. You know that hunk of junk is his baby," she said as she reached for another cigarette seconds after snuffing out the first.

Glenn did love his truck. He worked on at every weekend. It had definitely seen better days, but at least it ran. To him, that was all that mattered.

"I know," I said. Farah wiggled in her sleep, and I knew it was because the stroller had come to a standstill. If I didn't get up and start moving them around, the twins were bound to wake. Catnaps only made them grouchy. "Have you talked to anyone else?" I stood and walked to the stroller. I released the brake and moved it back and forth as I stayed in place, staring at Taryn.

"Of course I have. Everyone I thought he might have talked to by now or could be staying with. No one has heard from him. No one has seen him." She took another drag off her cigarette and exhaled the smoke upward so it wouldn't go in the twins' faces. I didn't think it mattered where she blew her smoke. I could still smell the cigarette from here. It saturated the air around us. "I don't know what to do. I love him, Mina. If something happened to him..."

"Nothing happened to him." I wasn't sure why the words spurred from my mouth, especially considering the things I knew. "Everything will be okay. He'll come back. You have to stay positive."

"It's hard to stay positive when no one believes me. You're the first person who's actually heard me out. Candace didn't even want to hear it. She doesn't think we're good together. If you ask me though, I think she's jealous of our relationship."

I didn't think that was it. I just thought Candace wanted better for her sister. She wanted more than this trailer park for her. She wanted more than Mirror Lake.

Candace had gotten out of town the second Taryn graduated high school, and she never looked back. She left the pack. She left her hometown. She left her sister. I liked to think it was because she moved on to bigger and better things, but I couldn't imagine leaving behind my own family for selfish gain.

Farah stirred in her seat again. Her tiny legs extended, kicking her brother in the process. He stirred as well, and I debated reaching for the lavender spray Gran had given me. Maybe a squirt on their T-shirts would make them sleep a little longer.

I couldn't bring myself to do it, though.

"I should get going," I said as a rocked the stroller a little harder. "I'm pretty sure these two are about to wake up, and when they do, you can bet they'll want something to eat." Their appetites never ceased to amaze me.

"You're probably right about that." Taryn's gaze drifted to the twins. "It's fine. I think I'm going to take a trip to the woods to see if I can find Glenn anyway."

"No!" I shouted, startling her. Taryn didn't need to go into the woods. If she did, she might find the area of blood I'd found. In her frame of mind, it might be best if she didn't see that. "Trekking through the woods by yourself isn't smart. You know what my Gran always says."

"I know, but sitting here doing nothing isn't smart either. What if something happened to him out there? What if he's hurt? I should be out there looking for him since nobody else gives a damn or believes me." Her words were harsh and sharp. I let her tone wash over me, knowing I would feel exactly the way she did if the shoe were on the other foot. On the other hand, I didn't blame anyone for not believing her. Taryn and Glenn were always fighting about something. They were the most on-again, off-again couple I'd ever known. "Westley didn't even want to hear it, and he's our damn Alpha."

What could I say that would keep her out of the woods?

I didn't want to give her any information until I had something concrete, but I had to give her something to keep her away from the place Glenn was probably attacked and abducted.

I tried to think of something, but nothing would come. Farah started to whine. Her chubby arms flailed about. Rocking the stroller back and forth wasn't working. Farah needed to feel the bumping of the gravel. Either that or she needed her diaper changed.

Taryn's cell rang. She glanced at the screen with wild hope festering in her eyes, but the second she processed the name and number it died. "It's my sister. I should probably take this."

"That's fine. Like I said, the twins are going to be hungry little beasts when they wake. I'll ask around, though, see if anyone has seen Glenn for you. Let them know you haven't seen him since Friday night."

"Get back with me if you learn anything, please," she pleaded.

"I will."

Taryn pressed a button on her cell and answered her sister's call. "Calling to apologize?"

I couldn't hear her sister's reply, but whatever it was, it made Taryn cry again.

"I'd love for you to come. I need you here. Thank you," she said.

My heart warmed. Candace was coming for a visit. Maybe she wasn't as cold-hearted and selfish as I'd once thought.

I started toward Felicia's place. Sweat beaded across my

brow. Maybe the twins were waking up because it was so humid out already. AC might calm them down.

A car cruised past me, kicking up dust from the gravel. I glanced over my shoulder, checking for more traffic and caught sight of Eli's new place.

I really needed to talk to him.

I spun the stroller around and headed toward his trailer. Taryn was still on the phone with her sister when I passed. I wondered when Candace would be able to get here and what she'd tell Taryn they should do since the police didn't seem to be offering any help.

Eli's truck wasn't there when I rounded his place. Disappointment crashed through me. I'd been hoping he'd be home so I could fill him in on everything I'd learned, along with my new theory on who I'd seen in the woods. I fished my cell out of my back pocket and scrolled through my contacts until I found his name. A new text came through from Alec before I could tap on Eli's name.

Got any plans for the night? I was thinking we could try that movie thing again.

It was Alec. Crap. I couldn't go to the movies with him tonight. There was too much going on here. Too much I needed to fill Eli in on.

Hey, sorry but I can't. I promised my Gran I'd help her with something. – Mina

I hated lying to Alec, but I didn't have a choice. Not if I wanted to meet up with Eli later tonight to discuss what I'd found out. It would be strictly pack business this time. No moonshine. No helping with his projects around the trailer.

At least that was what I was telling myself to make me feel less guilty.

Okay. Maybe later this week, then. I want to see you.

My heart pitter-pattered faster in my chest. I wanted to see Alec, too. Sunday seemed forever ago.

I want to see you, too. Later this week we can hang out for sure. – Mina

Regardless of what happened with this whole Glenn thing, I definitely needed to carve out time for Alec. I craved the normalcy of his presence and his sweet southern manners.

I switched gears and opened up a new message by tapping on Eli's name.

Hey, I need to talk to you. Are you working? – Mina

When Eli didn't respond as quickly as I would've liked, I turned the stroller around and headed back to Felisha's place. Farah was totally awake and Fletcher wasn't far behind. He kept grunting. Either he was slowly waking or taking a dump. Either was plausible.

When I reached Felicia's trailer and bent to scoop Farah out of the stroller, my cell chimed with a new text. I ignored it and got the twins out. Once I made it inside and settled them on the beanbag chair they seemed to adore, I reached for my phone. It was from Eli.

Of course, I'm a workin' man. What do we need to talk about?

Remember when I told you what I saw in the woods Sunday? – Mina

Yeah.

Well, I think it has something to do with Glenn. Can we meet up tonight sometime so I can fill you in on everything I learned today? – Mina

Sure. I should be done with this landscaping job around six. Then I have to head to the bar to help Eddie restock the shelves. We had an order come in today.

Dang, he was busy. I knew he worked hard, but I didn't realize he worked that hard.

How long will that take you? – Mina

Not long. I should be home before nine.

I'll meet you at your place, then. – Mina

You bringing dinner, or should I?

I scoffed. Who said anything about food?

I'm not bringing you anything. – Mina

Don't worry, seeing you after a long day of work will be enough.

My thumbs hovered over the keys of my phone as I debated on how I should respond. In the end, I decided not to say anything. I chose to ignore the way Eli's words made me feel, too. However, I couldn't ignore the fact I'd turned down a movie with Alec to spend time with Eli instead.

Pack business. That's all it was. Right?

12

L ights were on at Eli's place, but he wasn't answering his door. Was I supposed to let myself in? Or should I knock again?

As I debated what to do, the door swung open, startling me. I opened my mouth to say something, but bit back my words the second I noticed Eli was before me almost naked.

He stared down at me from where I was on the second step with a look of amusement flickering in his green eyes. He wore nothing besides a tattered towel draped around his waist and a smirk. My lungs forgot how to breathe. My heart forgot how to beat. All I could do was stare.

"Sorry. I thought I'd have enough time to jump in the shower before you got here," Eli said as water dripped from him. Droplets landed on my forearm jolting me awake from the trance I'd been put under at the sight of him. "Let me get dressed and then you can fill me in on everything." He stepped to the side so I could come in. My legs wobbled beneath me as I climbed the remaining steps.

Words wouldn't come. I watched his retreating form, practically salivating. His skin had grown darker since the last time I'd seen him, and I knew it was because he'd been working outside. Shirtless. There wasn't a single tan line across his back. In fact, the upper portion was blood red from too much sun.

"You should really put some aloe on. It looks like you got a bad burn today," I called down the hall after him, grateful I'd been able to find my voice at all.

"Tell me about it," he shouted back. "I'm definitely feeling it."

"Gran makes a spray and a salve with aloe. I can get something for you if you want it."

Eli stepped into sight, tugging on a white cotton T-shirt. He'd pulled on a pair of khaki cargo shorts, but no shoes. His hair was still dripping wet and disheveled. From where I stood, I could see droplets sliding down his neck and wetting the collar of his shirt.

"Nah, I'll be fine. You know as well as I do this will be gone by tomorrow morning," he said.

The whole Moon Kissed thing did have its perks. "Right."

"So, what's this about Glenn?" Eli asked as he stepped into the kitchen and opened the cabinet beside the refrigerator.

I knew what he was going for—the moonshine he always kept there. I wondered if he was still drinking the apple pie batch from the other night, or if he'd bought something else. Not that it mattered. I wouldn't be drinking with him again. Not after what almost happened last time.

I had enough guilt pressing down on me. I didn't need to add any more.

"Long story short, I overheard part of a phone conversation Taryn was having earlier. She was telling her sister she thought Glenn was missing. Apparently, they'd been drinking and got into an argument. She took his keys so he wouldn't drive away, and instead, he shifted and hauled ass to the woods," I paused, watching as Eli took a healthy swig of moonshine. His Adam's apple bobbed in the process. I waited for him to pass the jar to me next, but he didn't. "That was on Friday night. She claims she hasn't seen him since."

"Has anyone?" Eli's brows furrowed.

"According to her, no."

"You think the wolf in the woods Friday night was Glenn?"

"Yeah, I do."

Eli smoothed a hand over his face. "Did she talk to my dad?"

"Yeah, sorry to say it, but he wasn't much help to her either."

"They fight too much for her fears to hold any clout. Plus, he's been busy with something else," he said as he scratched at his brow.

The mysterious words caused the fine hairs on the back of my neck to stand on end. "Oh?"

Eli ignored my question. Probably because whatever it was his dad was busy with was pack related, and Eli wasn't at liberty to tell me. "Did Taryn call around at all?"

"Yeah, no luck. She filed a police report labeling him as a missing person, too."

"I'm sure that didn't do a damn bit of good." Eli took another swig of moonshine. He held it out to me afterward this time. "Want some?"

I shook my head. "No, I'm good."

"Oh, come on," he pressed. "I can tell you want it."

I rolled my eyes. "Whatever."

"It's true. Desire for it is oozing from you."

His words had my heart stalling in my chest. It wasn't the moonshine I was desiring.

"Take it," he said as he inched the jar closer to me. "Just one sip."

I took it from him and sighed. "You do realize you're contributing to a minor, right? I'm only eighteen."

Eli shrugged. "I know. And I think saying someone has to be twenty-one before they can drink legally is bullshit."

I placed the jar to my lips and willed myself to take a swig of the stout-smelling liquid. Fire coated my throat instantly, but it wasn't as potent as the last time. Was I already building up a tolerance to the stuff?

"Why is that?" I choked out the words and flew into a coughing fit.

Nope. Hadn't built up a tolerance yet.

"Because if a person can legally go to war, ready to die for this country, I think they should be able to buy themselves a damn drink legally."

He had a point. "I've never thought of it like that." My tongue felt numb as I handed the jar back to him. I leaned against the kitchen counter. "But, to get back to what we were talking about before, no. Filing a police report didn't do anything to help. They didn't send out a search party or anything. All they told Taryn was that he'd come back when he had cooled off enough."

"Figures. She probably would have been better off if she

hadn't mentioned the argument at all," Eli said as he hoisted himself onto the countertop.

I did the same and noticed when he set the mason jar between us. "Yeah, but then she'd look guilty or like she had something to do with his disappearance, wouldn't she?"

"Maybe, but they also might look further into the whole thing."

"Candace is coming, so I'm sure they'll be looking into things a lot harder soon. You know how she can be," I said.

"Candace? Jesus, Mirror Lake had better watch out."

"She was a real piece of work, wasn't she?"

"Hell yeah, she was. Can't believe she's stepping foot in town again." Eli reached for a bag of tortilla chips near him. The bag crinkled as he opened it. It was loud, but it was nothing compared to the sound of him crunching on the chips next to me. I couldn't stand hearing someone eat, especially when it was something crunchy. "You know, I used to have a thing for Candace."

His sudden admittance surprised me enough to make me deaf to the sound of him eating. "Really?"

"Yeah, why not? She was pretty, smart, driven. All the qualities any man would want in a woman."

"Yeah, but..." I stalled as I tried to think of a nice way to tell him they were the exact opposite of each other. "Y'all have nothing in common. And I do mean nothing. Candace was pretty, smart, and driven, but she was also hoity-toity and high maintenance. Definitely not someone I'd ever picture you with."

"Is that so?"

I nodded. "I can't believe you ever thought you had a shot with her."

"Never said I thought I had a shot with her. All I said was that I used to have a thing for her." Eli reached into the bag of chips and pulled out another handful of crumbs. "If you don't picture me with someone high maintenance and hoity-toity, as you put it, then who do you picture me with?"

My mouth grew dry. He'd put me on the spot. Who did I picture Eli with? Honestly?

Me.

I was the first person to come to mind when I thought of him being with anyone. It was wrong of me, so wrong of me, but it didn't change the truth to it.

What the hell? Where was all that distance I used to keep between us? How could I be having thoughts like that about him?

"I, uh," I fumbled for words as I tried to think of anyone who might be a decent match for him. No one came to mind.

"Someone like you maybe?" His lips curled into a half smile.

My heart thundered against my rib cage, making it hard for me to breathe. He had to hear it. It was so loud it was the only thing I could hear.

"No." I squeezed my eyes shut. My voice was too breathy sounding. It caused my heart to pound so hard my fingertips tingled. "I don't know. All I'm saying is that Candace isn't your type."

"Glad you know my type so much better than I do," he said. His words weren't harsh, but they still had an effect on me. I opened my eyes to glance at him. He held the bag of chips out. "Want some?"

"If you had guacamole, yeah. I can't eat them plain like that, though. It's gross." My nose wrinkled with disgust, but secretly, I was glad we were talking about something else. The conversation had steered into dangerous territory.

"How is it gross? It's salted chips," Eli said. He stared at me as though I'd grown two heads.

"Anyway," I dragged the word out and reached for the jar of moonshine. "I have a hunch about what might have happened to Glenn."

"Yeah?"

"I've got a feeling Alec's friend, Shane, and his brothers took him," I said before placing the jar to my lips. It didn't burn nearly as bad this time. In fact, it went down smoothly. Apple pie moonshine was all right. "I told you they hunt there year-round. Becca said they were out there Friday night, the same night I heard a wolf in the woods and the same night Taryn and Glenn fought."

Eli reached for the moonshine; his fingertips brushed against mine in the process. Warmth bloomed through my lower stomach. I blamed it on the alcohol kicking in, but knew that wasn't entirely true.

"I hate people who hunt year-round," he said.

"I hate Taryn is having to go through this."

Eli glanced at me. "We should do something about it."

"Like what?"

It wasn't that I didn't want to do something; it was that I wasn't sure what we could do. Contacting the police had already been done. Letting the Alpha of the pack know what was going on had already been done. Wasn't that all you were supposed to do in a situation like this? It wasn't as though I could head to the police station and tell them Glenn changed into a wolf from time to time, and I thought Shane and his brothers might have kidnapped him last Friday night during one of his shifts. They'd think I was nuts. On the other hand, I couldn't barge into Eli's dad's place and demand he do something to help either.

"We should head to the woods and search for clues," Eli said as he took another swig of moonshine. "It's our duty, don't you think? I mean, after all, we know more than the police at this point and my father is busy with other things. Maybe we need to take this situation into our own hands. After all, it is pack related."

I thought about what he was saying for a minute. "I think you're right."

"Damn." Eli chuckled. "I never thought I'd hear you say those words to me."

I slapped him on the shoulder. Moonshine splashed on the kitchen floor when I jostled him. It wasn't much, but it was enough to make me laugh.

"What's so funny? That's alcohol abuse. I should totally cut you off," Eli insisted with a grin.

"It is alcohol abuse, but it's funny because the only thing I could think about was how that's probably the cleanest spot on your floor. That moonshine is so potent it could kill anything it comes in contact with."

"You're probably right." Eli chuckled.

While I wasn't smashed, I was feeling tipsy. Eli had to be, too. I could tell from the glossy sheen to his eyes.

"You ready to take a hike through the woods and crack this case?" he asked, pulling me from my thoughts.

"Yeah," I said, slipping off the counter. I landed on my feet and a puff of white floated up from the floor. Drywall dust was everywhere. I wiped off my bottom, sending more flying through the air. The countertop was covered in it. "Great, my butt is probably all chalky."

"Turn around, let me see," Eli said as he spun his index finger around in the air, signaling me to do as he said.

"Not a chance." I knew he was only using the moment as an excuse to check out my ass. It sent a shiver through me that was hard to ignore, but I managed. "Come on; let me show you where I found the blood."

Eli slipped off the counter without worrying about dusting his bottom off. "Whoa there, let's get some supplies first."

"Supplies? Like what?"

"Well, I for one don't plan on using the flashlight on my cell phone. We'll cover more ground if we have something with a wider range to it."

"What are you planning on using, a freaking lighthouse?" The flashlight on my cell was perfect. I didn't need anything else.

"No, but I have a good flashlight we can use. Plus, I should probably change into something else. You too," he said, taking in what I was wearing.

The feel of his eyes on me had my stomach flip-flopping again. I glanced at my clothes, hoping to take my mind off the way he was looking at me. I had on my favorite pair of cut-off shorts and a white tank top with *messy hair don't care* printed in black cursive lettering on the front. "What's wrong with what I'm wearing?"

"You're going to stick out like a sore thumb in the dark."

"What are you suggesting? I go home and change into something black so we can hit the woods in ninja mode?"

"Something like that, minus the you heading home part."

He started toward the back of his trailer. My gaze drifted to his dust-covered bottom. Lord, he was good-looking. "Come on. Let me see if I have anything black you can wear."

I trailed behind Eli, heading down the narrow hallway with excitement sparking through my system at the thought of being in his bedroom. Immediately, I scolded myself for thinking that way. This was pack business. Even though I wasn't Moon Kissed, this was still my pack. It always would be. No matter what. I wasn't going into Eli's bedroom to make out with him and do the dirty. I was going to prepare for a mission. I'd take him to the spot I saw the blood and we'd look for clues that might help us find Glenn. Nothing more, nothing less.

13

Moonlight filtered through the cloudy sky. It illuminated sections of the woods around us, but not enough for me to see without the help of added light. Even so, I knew finding my way to the track wouldn't be hard. Usually, I went straight from the trailer park to the lake along the path I'd carved out years ago, but I remembered the track being to the right of my usual path.

"It shouldn't be too much farther," I whispered to Eli. He walked beside me, dressed in all black.

"Really? That's too close to home for me."

My stomach churned. I'd never thought about how Alec's uncle's piece of property was so close to where we lived. That meant Shane and his brothers had been hunting in our backyard for who knew how long. The other night might not have been their first abduction, or kill, however you wanted to look at it.

Gran's warning of never running alone echoed through my mind. Would Glenn still have been abducted if he'd been

140

with someone else that night? Would he have been shot? I wasn't sure. All I knew was, if I became Moon Kissed, there wasn't a chance in hell I'd be caught running through these woods alone in wolf form.

"I know," I whispered. My throat was dry, causing my voice to sound hoarse as I swiped a low-hanging tree branch out of my way. It slipped from my grip and shot back, popping me in the arm and snagging the sleeve of Eli's T-shirt he'd loaned me for this expedition. It was only a work shirt, but it was soft and smelled of him. I didn't want it ruined for those reasons alone.

Eli's hand gripped my forearm. The warmth of his touch jolted each of my nerve endings to life. "Hold on a second," he whispered.

I paused and held my breath, unsure what had garnered his attention. "What is it?"

"Shhh," he insisted, placing a finger to his lips. "Cut your flashlight off and listen."

I swiped the flashlight on my cell off and strained my ears to hear what he did. There was nothing there. At least to my ears. Eli's hearing might be a smidgen better than mine, but not much. Not in this form. Only in his wolf form would he be able to hear exceptionally well.

Leaves rustled from a few feet away. The fine hairs at the nape of my neck and along my arms lifted as I jerked my attention toward the noise. My heart thundered against my rib cage as it grew closer. What if it was Shane, or one of his brothers? What if they shot us for snooping? I knew it wasn't their property, but I also knew that hadn't stopped them from shooting things here before.

"Just a rabbit," Eli whispered as he pointed to a thorny

bush to my left. A brown rabbit lunged inside it, disappearing beneath its prickly branches.

I clasped my chest, hoping to slow the erratic beating of my heart. "Just a heart attack waiting to happen, Jesus."

"You okay?" Amusement laced his words. I didn't have to see his face to know a ghost of a smile tugged at the corners of his lips.

"I'm fine." I flipped my flashlight back on and continued walking, this time paying more attention to my surroundings. We had to be close. Seriously, how could we miss a giant dirt track in the middle of the woods? Maybe that wasn't the best question to ask, considering I'd done so for years. "It should be here."

"I think you're right," Eli surprised me by saying. I thought he'd have razzed me for getting him lost in the woods, but he hadn't.

"How do you know?"

"Because I can see it," he insisted, pointing straight ahead. "If you weren't so vertically challenged, you might be able to see it from the top of this hill too."

"Whatever." I rolled my eyes even though he couldn't see me.

A few more steps forward and the dirt track came into view. Moonlight glinted over the man-made hills and valleys.

"You rode around this track on a four-wheeler?" Eli asked. I didn't miss the shock lacing his words.

"Yeah," I said as I placed a hand on my hip and shifted to glare at him, proud of myself. "Quite a few times actually."

"By yourself?"

"Yep."

"Huh, I never would have pictured you as a four-wheeling kind of girl."

"What kind of girl did you picture me as?" I asked before I'd had a chance to think the words through.

"Not the four-wheeling type, more like hike through nature or rock climbing. You've never crossed me as one of those adrenaline junkies who get off on four-wheeling, dirt biking, or skydiving."

I'd never pictured myself as that type of girl either. Then again, I'd never had the opportunity to do any of those things. So, who knew, I might be that girl after all.

"Maybe you don't know me as well as you thought you did," I said as I started toward the tree I remembered seeing the blood behind.

"Maybe, but I doubt it," I heard Eli mutter as he followed me through the brush.

There was such confidence in his voice that baffled me. How could a person think they knew someone else so well?

"This is the tree," I said as I shined my light on it. "The blood was behind it."

I swept my flashlight across the ground as I stepped around the tree. The ground was still roughed up from signs of a struggle, but the darkened splotches of crimson captured my attention. Now that I knew whom they potentially belonged to, bile crept up the back of my throat.

"That's definitely blood." Eli stepped into my light and bent down. I inched forward and watched as he touched the blood on one of the leaves. It flaked off and fell to the ground. He pointed to the claw marks and paw prints in the dirt. "And these are definitely from a wolf. I think you're right. Something bad did go down here."

Normally, I'd enjoy being right. This wasn't one of those times. I'd hoped Glenn had been blowing off steam still and would come home on his own, but it was clear that wasn't the case. While we didn't have any proof Glenn was the wolf taken by Shane and his brothers, the evidence was leaning toward it.

Eli stood and spun around to survey the area. "It's obvious they took him somewhere. There isn't a body. Glenn would have transformed into his human state once he was wounded, and it's safe to say from the amount of blood here, he was severely wounded. Since we know the guys you mentioned are hunters, I'm willing to bet it was a gunshot wound. Did you hear a gun go off that night?"

I licked my lips and thought back. "No."

I couldn't be sure, though. I'd been preoccupied with Alec. Had there been a shot fired?

"Maybe they used a silencer," Eli said.

The thought terrified me. It meant you would never hear the shot coming.

Eli shifted to face me. "If Shane and his brothers were the ones who did this to Glenn, then it means they know about us. Not that they suspect, but that they know. They would have proof of our existence. This isn't good." He smoothed his hands over his short-cropped hair.

"I know." I bit my bottom lip.

"It means Shane might know about you," Eli insisted. I could feel his eyes on me, but I couldn't bring myself to meet his gaze. Instead, I continued to stare at the last place Glenn was probably seen. "This is just another reason I think you should stay away from Alec." The way he said his name sounded as though it left a bad taste in his mouth.

I glanced at him. His jaw worked back and forth as he held my gaze, worry festering in his eyes.

"I'm serious," he spat. "I think it's time you tell that boy goodbye for good. No more screwing around."

My temper flared. Who did he think he was telling me I needed to say goodbye to someone? Who was he to say I was screwing with anyone either? He didn't know the specifics of how I felt about Alec. "He has nothing to do with this."

"Maybe, but his best friend did. That says a lot about him, don't you think? I mean, haven't you ever heard the term guilty by association?"

"It doesn't apply to this situation. Alec is nothing like Shane." I meant it. Eli must've understood as much, or at the very least he knew I wouldn't budge on it, because his lips pressed into a thin line and he looked away.

"Fine, whatever. I'm not going to argue with you about this. I've said my peace. You can either listen or don't. It's up to you. Just promise me you'll be careful when you're around him. I don't want to end up out here searching for you and finding another scene like this." He gestured to the blood and scratched up ground, and flashed me a pained stare that tugged at my heartstrings.

"Okay," I said even though I didn't think Alec would do anything to hurt me. I was merely touched that Eli seemed to care so much about me.

Footfalls rustling through leaves in the distance had me on high alert. Eli placed his index finger to his lips and moved to position himself in front of me.

"Turn your flashlight off and get down," he insisted.

Voices traveled through the woods. My chest tightened as my breathing accelerated. I fumbled with the flashlight on my cell, unable to get it to switch off fast enough. Eli took it from me and killed the light. I closed my eyes and released the breath I'd been holding. Another murmur of voices floated to me. I couldn't make out what was said, but I could distinguish the voices were male.

Shit. Was it Shane and his brothers back for another round of shoot, snatch, and run?

"We should get out of here before someone mistakes us for an animal and shoots." My voice shook as I whispered the words to Eli.

We were dressed in black, hiding behind brush—we were practically begging for a trigger-happy hunter to shoot us.

"One minute," Eli muttered, keeping his eyes trained forward. "Maybe we can get some clues about what they did with Glenn, or if it was intentional, by listening to them."

I had no doubt it was intentional. Eli didn't know Shane like I did. In fact, he didn't know him at all. Maybe this was where I should put my foot down and get us the hell out of here.

"I don't think sticking around is a good idea," I whispered.

He pretended he didn't hear me. At least that's what I thought he was doing, because he damn sure didn't turn around and acknowledge I'd spoken.

"Honestly, Drew, I don't know why you're dragging me out here tonight. Peter didn't ask for another one. He already has the filthy werewolf we bagged the other night. He doesn't need another," the guy's familiar voice sent chills creeping along my spine.

It was Shane. There was no doubt in my mind.

"Chill out. I don't know why I even brought you tonight.

You're such a damn wuss," Drew said in a sharp tone. I assumed he was one of Shane's older brothers.

"I'm not a wuss. I'm here, aren't I? I was here the other night and the times before that, too. And these aren't freaking wolves. They're *werewolves*. There's a damn difference," Shane said. He sounded closer. We were truly at risk of being shot if we didn't get out of here soon.

"Which is why we're out here," Drew said, sounding as though he was talking to a five-year-old. "I want to nab another one. I told you I can get a shit ton of money if I grab a female this time around."

"So you've said a million times. I don't see why you won't tell me who the guy is you're working with. What does he want with werewolves anyway?" Shane asked. The light on his flashlight skimmed the bush beside where Eli and I were crouched.

My hand snaked out and fisted the back of Eli's shirt in an ill-fated attempt to steady my trembling body.

"Don't know. Don't care. All I know is I'll be set for a while from the cash once I do," Drew said. "Now be quiet. If there's anything out here, you've probably done scared it away by now with your constant yapping."

"Yeah, like one of those things would be scared of us," Shane scoffed.

The click of a rifle being cocked echoed through the woods. "They will be once they see this baby."

"No doubt. Man, that thing is a beauty," Shane said. He spun around, aiming his flashlight in the opposite direction. I wasn't sure if something had caught his eye, or if he was continuing with his survey of the area. Either way, I was glad he wasn't looking near us anymore.

I loosened my grip on Eli's shirt. His hand found mine in the dark, and his warm touch settled over me like a sedative.

"All right," Eli whispered. His hot breath slipped along my clammy skin, stirring things to life inside me that didn't have any business being awoken in the moment. "Let's get out of here."

I nodded, glad to finally hear the words slip from his mouth. I'd heard enough. Knowing Drew had someone lined up to pay him for a female from our pack was sickening.

Eli's grip on my hand tightened as he eased us away from the two goons. We were still hunkered down in a crouched position, which made me feel safer but not safe enough.

Once there was enough distance between them and us, we righted ourselves to standing. Eli didn't let go of my hand right away, but maybe it was because I wouldn't let him. His touch was the only thing keeping me grounded in the moment. When he released a long breath, I glanced at him. The look plastered on his face let me know he was having a difficult time walking away. He wanted to go back. I could sense the anger he felt toward them. It rippled off him in waves now that I was focused on more than the feel of his hand in mine.

"I should go back and pummel them," Eli snarled, confirming my thoughts.

"No, you shouldn't. They have guns. You don't."

"I can shift. They won't know I'm coming."

"Being in wolf form didn't help Glenn any," I reminded him as we stepped into the clearing of the trailer park.

We'd made it back safely. Thank goodness.

I knew I should release Eli's hand and head home, but a part of me didn't want to. A larger part said I needed to make sure Eli calmed down enough so he wouldn't do anything stupid like go after them the second I left his side.

That was the part I listened to.

I tightened my grip on his hand and steered us toward his trailer. He didn't fight me. Heck, he didn't even seem to notice we were still holding hands.

"Glenn was a damn fool," Eli growled. "Everyone knows it's not safe to shift when you've been drinking."

"Right there. You need to heed your own advice."

Eli glared at me. "What are you talking about? I'm not even buzzed anymore. Seeing those guys and hearing what they said sobered me up quick."

I knew what he meant. I'd grown stone sober the second I heard Shane's voice. "Doesn't matter. It's not a good idea."

"Something needs to be done, though. We can't let them get away with this," he said in a low growl, his teeth gritting together.

We continued toward his trailer.

"I know, but I think we need more time to figure out what's really going on." Maybe it wasn't the smartest move, but it was all I could think to do. Charging after Shane and his brothers wasn't going to bring Glenn back. It wasn't going to help us figure this situation out either. While we might know something—like who was responsible—we didn't know enough. "We need to keep tabs on Shane and his brothers so we can learn where he took Glenn. We should probably watch the other members of the pack, especially the females, too."

Eli paused at the stairs leading to his front door. "Watch what? Watch as one of them gets abducted like Glenn did?" Eli snapped in a harsh whisper.

I knew he was pissed at the situation, not me, but I couldn't help but feel a sting of hurt at his words.

I chewed my bottom lip, hating what I was about to say next because I knew he wouldn't like it. "Maybe."

"No! I'm not about to sit back and let something like that happen to someone else," Eli insisted. He jerked his hand from mine. The sudden loss of his touch tingled across my palm. "You heard what that Shane guy said. He said he was there the other night and the times before that too. They could have nabbed more than just Glenn."

I'd heard, but I hadn't given much thought to it.

"All I meant was that maybe we could scout the woods or set up some bait for them so we can follow and see where they're taking them. Maybe it would lead us to Glenn. If not, then at least it would lead us to where he'd been taken and we can take the place down. You can't take a place down when you don't know where it's at." I started up the wooden stairs that led to his front door and let myself inside.

Who knew who was watching us and possibly over-hearing our conversation? We didn't know enough yet to pull others in. It would only cause more harm than good at this point. Panic was never anyone's friend.

"You know," Eli said as he started up the stairs behind me. "That's actually a good idea."

I headed for his kitchen. My mouth was bone dry. Stress always had that effect on me. "Of course it is. I came up with it."

Eli laughed. It was the reaction I was shooting for. It meant he was calming down. I was glad.

I opened the cabinet closest to the sink, searching for a cup. It was empty. "Got a cup?"

"No, but there's bottled water in the fridge." He closed the front door behind him and headed straight for me. I froze. He bypassed me and pulled a box of something down from a cabinet near my head. "You hungry at all?"

I moved around him in the tiny kitchen and grabbed a bottled water from the fridge. "Sort of." Judging from the lack of food in his fridge, I didn't think he had much to spare, though. "Depends on what you're making,"

"Mac and cheese." He placed a pot filled with water on the stove and cranked one of the burners to high. The water would be boiling in seconds, and once he added in the pasta, it was sure to bubble over. "I've been living off that and scrambled eggs for days."

"Seriously?" Gran would have heart failure if she knew. His mom probably would, too. "Why haven't you gone home for at least one nice meal?"

He shrugged and dumped the pasta in before the water had a chance to warm. "I don't know. Call it pride, call it whatever you want, I don't want to have to go home for anything. I want my parents to know I can do this on my own. Besides, it's not bad if you cook the noodles right. I can't stand it when they get mushy, and I happen to like eggs."

"Going home for one meal a week is not proof you can't live on your own. It's called quality time with your family," I insisted as I hoisted myself on the counter and opened my bottle of water.

There still wasn't a scrap of furniture in the place with the exception of the bed and rickety dresser in his room. I imagined both had been his when he lived with his parents.

"Maybe," he said as he reached for a wooden spoon that

looked as though he'd chiseled it himself and stirred the noodles.

Silence built between us. It was awkward and tense. It had me questioning whether I should still be here. Eli wasn't going after Shane or Drew; he was making mac and cheese. I should probably leave, but I didn't want to.

If I directed our conversation back to stuff involving Glenn and the pack, then it counted as pack business and I was allowed to stay, right?

"So, I'm supposed to hang out with Alec sometime this week. It would be the perfect opportunity for me to hang around Shane and ask some questions about his brothers. Anything we can learn about him and his family might be valuable. It might lead us to Glenn and help put a stop to whatever they're doing."

"I don't like the idea of you hanging around him. I know I said I didn't care for you hanging around Alec to begin with, but this is serious, Mina. The full moon is coming. That means you're going to have to drink the tea again. If it triggers a reaction this time, you'll be Moon Kissed. Which means you'll be a prime target for Shane and his brothers."

"It might not happen, though. It hasn't yet," I insisted. At this point, I was beginning to think it might never happen.

"It will. I can sense it," Eli said as he shifted to face me. "I've always been able to sense it in you." His smoldering eyes pulled me in.

The moment was becoming too intimate, which exactly what I'd been trying to avoid. I averted my gaze, even though it was the last thing I wanted to do.

"Only time will tell," I whispered, unsure what else to say.

Eli stepped toward me. Something in the air shifted as he continued to erase the space previously separating us. I lifted my gaze to meet his and caught sight of a dangerous glimmer sparking to life within the color of his eyes.

Eli was about to kiss me.

His lips were about to press against mine. It was written all over his face. My heart stalled out when only inches remained between us. His gaze locked with mine as the charge in the air intensified due to our close proximity. I was frozen, waiting to see what would happen next.

An eruption of something sizzling burst through the trailer, startling me and causing Eli to spin around to find its source. Steam billowed to the ceiling coming from the stove. Eli rushed to remove the pot he'd been boiling his noodles in from the burner.

"Damn it," he growled. "Now the noodles will be mushy."

"That's not your only problem," I said as I brought my hand up to cover my nose. "The stench of burned water is going to linger for a while."

He set the pot back down on the stove. "It does have a distinct smell, doesn't it? Maybe when I add in the cheese it'll be okay."

I hopped off the counter and stepped to the nearest window. "I'm not taking any chances. It could just make it worse."

Once I had the window open, I went for the front door and fanned it to get more fresh air inside faster. I caught sight of Gracie and Cooper together. Their heads were close. In fact, from this angle, it looked as though they were making out.

"Since when is your brother dating my sister?" My tone was harsh. There was no denying how unhappy I was about the situation.

"Whoa." Eli stopped what he was doing and shifted to face me. "I know nothing about that. Which brother is she dating?"

"Cooper. Which one do you think she'd go for, Jonas? He's nine."

"She's thirteen. It's only a four-year difference. I've seen bigger age gaps between people before." Eli went back to his noodles. He drained the pasta and then rummaged through the fridge for whatever else mac and cheese called for.

I poked my head out the door to get a better look at my sister and Cooper. Her arms were wrapped around his neck. His hands were gripping her hips. Their faces were still stuck together.

"They're making out! I can't believe my little sister is making out with someone. She's doing it right there in the open for anyone to see, too." I shook my head, appalled by what I was seeing. "I need to have words with her. Soon."

"Why? Because dating a Vargas boy is so bad?"

My teeth grazed over my bottom lip as I thought about how my words might have come off. I stepped away from the door. "That's not what I'm saying. I'm just saying..." What was I saying? Why did Gracie dating Cooper bother me so much? Was it that she was dating him specifically, or that she was dating in general? That was it. "This is Gracie. My *little* sister. She shouldn't be kissing boys at all."

Gracie was thirteen. She was too young to be doing something like that. Hell, she was too young to be interested in boys. Too young for boys to be interested in her.

"And? Cooper is my little brother," Eli said with his back still to me. He poured milk into the pot of noodles and stirred. "What are you so worried about? They're thirteen. Dating was bound to happen. At least she picked one of the pack members to date." I didn't care for the edge to his words.

"What's that supposed to mean?" I knew it was a jab at me for dating Alec, but I wanted to hear him say it.

"Nothing," he said with a shrug. "Look, don't worry about it. Cooper is a good kid. So is Gracie. They'll be fine." He grabbed two paper plates from a cabinet and scooped mac and cheese onto them. "Here, eat something."

I exhaled a long breath. Gracie was a good kid. Cooper was, too. Neither of them had ever been in any trouble. Cooper had always creeped me out, though. I didn't like how he kept tabs on me with Eli's other brother, Tate. Maybe he was protective of those in the pack.

I walked to where Eli stood holding a paper plate filled with macaroni and took it from him. It had been forever since I'd eaten mac and cheese. Gran didn't buy it. Everything she cooked was homemade.

"Thanks," I said as I shoveled a forkful in my mouth. "You know, if you don't want to go home for a dinner, you could always come to my place. Gran would love to cook for you."

"What about you?"

"What about me?" I glanced at him.

"Would you cook for me?" he asked, not bothering to keep the heat from his words or his eyes.

The breath in my chest stilled as goose bumps erupted across my skin. "Umm, I'm not much of a cook. All I know how to make is canned tomato soup and grilled cheese."

"One of my favorite meals." Eli winked. "That would be great. Thanks."

What just happened? Did we agree on another meal together? Was I supposed to make him tomato soup and grilled cheese now? I wasn't sure.

All I knew was that if he mentioned it again, I didn't think I'd tell him no.

14

Sunlight beat down on me. It was a crisp ninety-six degrees today. I was guessing that was why Alec had set up a lake adventure. I enjoyed going to the lake regardless of the temperature, so I'd agreed to come along with him and his friends. It was the perfect way to spend a Saturday afternoon, especially one this close to a full moon. With only four nights left, I needed a distraction. Looming full moons always left me a little on edge.

Gran said becoming Moon Kissed wouldn't hurt, but no matter what she said, I wouldn't believe her. I had to experience it myself. She called me stubborn, but I said it was being smart. I didn't think a person should ever base anything in life on the way someone else perceived it.

"My nose is already starting to feel tight," Becca said, drawing my attention to her. She wrinkled her nose and reached for the bottle of sunblock beside her. We were sitting in the grassy area at the edge of the lake, soaking up some sun. "Am I getting red yet?"

"A little pink, but not red."

"You're so lucky. I wish I had skin that browned instead of burned. I think at this point, I've given up on ever having a good tan." She opened the bottle of sunblock and squirted some into her palm.

"There's always spray tans," I offered. "I've seen some that look pretty realistic. They don't look as orange as they used to."

"Tried it once. Hated it. You can't shower well while you have one. Plus, you have to leave it on your skin for like forever before you can shower the first time. It stained my sheets and made me look like an Oompa Loompa."

An image of the short, orange guys shifted through my head, causing me to chuckle. "Sorry, I'm not laughing at you. I swear."

"It's fine," Becca said as she held the bottle of sunblock out to me. "Think you could get my shoulders and back? Shane didn't do a good job. He doesn't understand that when I say I need a thick layer, I really mean it. One time last summer, I trusted him to put some on my back, and he did a really crappy job. I wound up with blisters. It was not fun."

I winced as I took the bottle from her. "Yikes, I can imagine."

I squeezed a dollop of sunblock into my hand and allowed my gaze to drift to where the guys were flopping around on inflatables in the water. I slathered the coconut-scented sunblock on Becca's back and the tops of her shoulders while I zeroed in on Shane. He wore dark sunglasses that blocked his eyes from my view. I couldn't be sure if he was looking at me now, but knew I'd felt his stare in the last few minutes. He was watching me. Dread pooled in my stomach.

Was he thinking of kidnapping me so his brother could sell me to whoever it was he'd been talking about the other night? Little did he know, I hadn't been Moon Kissed. Even if I had been, I'd like to see him try doing something like that to me. I'd take him out in a heartbeat. At five foot two, I might be a tiny thing, but that didn't mean I couldn't take care of myself. People always underestimated me because of my size.

Once I'd sucker punched a guy for slapping me on the ass when I walked past him at a party. He didn't bother me again that night. In fact, no one did.

"Thanks." Becca shifted around on her towel and reached into the bag beside her. She pulled out something square and handed it to me. "Here, for your hands."

"Oh, thanks," I said as I took the towelette from her.

A loud splash drew my attention to the boys. Benji had flipped the raft Shane was floating on over, sending him toppling into the water. My lips twisted into a smirk that was hard to dim. It was about time someone knocked him off his high horse.

Shane came up for air huffing and puffing. He was missing his sunglasses.

"Oh no. He's going to be so pissed," Becca said, shaking her head. "Those sunglasses cost him a hundred and forty dollars."

"Jesus. Why did he spend so much on sunglasses?" I'd never understood why people did that. They were the number one thing people either lost or broke over the summer.

Then again, maybe that was me.

"To show off." Becca rolled her eyes. I guess spending so much on sunglasses wasn't her thing either.

"Where did he even get that kind of money to blow?" If I had a hundred and forty dollars lying around, sunglasses would be the last thing I'd buy. I'd spend it all on my car. My two front tires were so bald I was waiting for them to blowout while I drove down the street. "Does he even have a job?"

"Not really. He does stuff for his brothers."

Bingo. This was the perfect opportunity to get more information out of Becca about Shane and his brothers. I couldn't pass it up.

"What kind of stuff? A hundred and forty dollars is a lot of money," I pressed.

Please bite. Please bite.

"I'm not sure. He doesn't talk about it a lot. I think it has something to do with hunting, though. Honestly," she said, her voice dipping to a whisper. "I think he's part of an underground hunting scheme. I'm pretty sure they make money selling meat and skins to people, as gross as it sounds."

My stomach churned. If she only knew how gross it actually did sound to me, considering what they'd been hunting lately.

"What the hell, man?" Shane shouted as he hoisted himself back onto his float.

I wanted to keep the conversation Becca and I were having rolling. It was important I got as much information out of her as I could while we were on the subject. "Is there really that much money to be made in...poaching?" It was a term I'd heard a time or two on one of the TV shows my dad watched.

Poaching. Was that what Shane and his brothers were doing with the members of the pack? It sounded like it.

"I guess. I know it's how Shane makes all his money. I don't know about his older brothers, though. His oldest brother, Peter, runs the vet clinic at the edge of town, but I'm not sure what Drew does to be honest." Becca pulled the cooler beside her closer. She opened the top and pulled two cans of soda out. "Here. Oh, are you hungry yet? I made BLT wraps this time," she said as she handed me a soda.

So, Peter was a vet? Or at least, he worked for one. What could he possibly want with someone from the pack? As for Drew, well I already knew how he made his money.

"Uh, yeah. I'll have one," I said. I opened my mouth to ask another question, but the sight of food being passed out had garnered the guys' attention.

They splashed to shore as the information Becca had given me looped through my mind on repeat. It stopped only when one question formed: If Peter was a vet, then why did he allow his younger brothers to shoot Glenn? Wouldn't it have been easier and less messy to use a tranquilizer instead? As a vet, or even just working in the office, he should have access to those.

"What do you have for us this time?" Alec asked Becca as he squeezed out his swimming trunks while walking toward us. Sunlight glistened off his tanned chest as water droplets trickled to the ground around him.

"BLT wraps." Becca beamed as she held up the one she was eating. "There's soda and chips, too."

"Shane you're one lucky man," Benji said as he smacked him on the back in passing. "I wish I could find a girl who cooked for me all the time."

"Why? So you could sit around on your fat ass and eat all day?" Shane asked.

Why did anyone hang around this guy? He was a complete jerk.

"Whatever. I ain't fat; I'm healthy," Benji said as he slapped his stomach.

"Says your mama." Shane laughed.

"Do you need anything?" Alec asked, nudging my leg.

"Um, sure. I'll take a bag of chips."

Alec grabbed two bags of chips, a wrap, and a soda. He situated himself on the corner of my towel, and I folded my legs beneath me to give him more room.

"I'm glad you came," Alec said with a wide smile as he opened my chips for me before handing them over. The sweet gesture didn't go unnoticed by me.

"Me too." I was. It felt like forever since I'd hung out with him. I'd missed him.

Our fingers brushed when I took my chips from him, causing tiny sparks of want to shimmer through me. My gaze trailed over him, taking in his rock-hard abs and toned arms.

"What are you doing tomorrow?" he asked, making my eyes snap to his.

"I'm supposed to babysit again. Felicia, the lady I babysat the twins for a couple days ago, is working another double. Sundays are good days for tips at the diner, apparently."

"Of course, everybody is starved by the time they get out of church," Benji said around a mouthful of food. "The last thing I want to do is go home and make myself somethin' to eat. You know food always tastes better when someone else cooks for you."

"You're welcome," Becca said, surprising me. I'd never heard her say something in such a teasing tone before.

"Thank you, Becca. These wraps are the shit." Benji grinned.

"Like I said, you're welcome," Becca said at the same time Alec asked me when I had to babysit till.

"I'm not sure. Most of the time her mom comes halfway through and picks the twins up when Felicia works a double." I popped one of the salty potato chips in my mouth. "It could be between four and five or a little later before I get off."

"Oh. I was thinking of heading to the track tomorrow afternoon once I get out of church."

"I'm down for that," Benji said.

Shane nodded. "Me too."

"If you get off at like four, you should come out to the track for a minute," Alec insisted.

"Okay, sure." Racing around the track a few times sounded fun.

"Oh, man. It's almost six already," Benji said as he glanced at his phone. "I need to scoot. I promised my dad I'd help him with some yard work."

"Yard work at six o'clock at night?" Shane asked. His skeptical tone was amusing, considering he was someone I'd found skeptical from the beginning.

"Not exactly. Dinner first. Then yard work." Benji downed the remainder of his soda.

"You just ate," Alec said.

"And?" Benji grinned. "I've never turned down one of my mom's meals. I don't plan on it either."

I waited for Shane to spout another fat joke, but he didn't.

Instead everyone tossed their trash in the cooler before gathering the floats they'd brought. I heard Shane say something to Benji about him owing him a pair of sunglasses, but I couldn't hear Benji's reply. I hoped it was something smart-ass. Shane deserved it.

"I should get going too," I said, slipping on my sandals. "I promised my grandma I'd help her in the garden. My sister was supposed to, but she's been preoccupied with a neighborhood boy lately." I rolled my eyes, still unable to get over Gracie and Cooper being an item.

"How old is your sister again?" Becca asked.

"Thirteen."

"Aw, how sweet."

"I guess." I sighed. Why didn't people understand this was my baby sister? The last thing I wanted her to do was date. Dating boys only lead to heartache. It would cause her pain, which was something I didn't want her to experience any more than she already had in her life.

"Wait. Is the guy older or something?" Becca asked. "You don't seem too happy about her dating him."

"No. He's thirteen, too."

"What's the problem, then? You don't like him?"

"It's not that I don't like him. I guess I just don't like the idea of her dating." I waited for her to tell me I was being too overprotective, but she didn't.

"Got ya," Becca surprised me by saying. "I felt the same way about my little sister. She's fifteen, though. Lots of drama and heartache I wish she didn't have to deal with. Doesn't work that way, though. We all have to experience things for ourselves, you know?"

I nodded. "Yeah."

The more I hung around Becca, the more I liked her. I'd never had a girlfriend before. I'd always pretty much been friendless. I was content hanging out with myself. Plus, I had Gran and Gracie. There was never any need to make friends beyond my family. Besides, I'd known from an early age things in the trailer park were different from beyond it. Making friends outside the park seemed like a waste of time because of it. Being Moon Kissed was sort of a friend deterrent.

Now that I wasn't sure it would ever happen, I guess I was open to new things. Dating Alec had been one of them. Becoming fast friends with Becca seemed like another.

"If you need any help tomorrow babysitting, let me know." Becca tossed a few pieces of trash the guys had missed into the cooler and closed the lid.

"Thanks," I said. "What's your number?"

She laughed as she reached for the edge of her towel. "Might be hard to get a hold of me if you don't have my number. Sorry, sometimes I get scatterbrained."

"It's fine." I pulled out my cell to input her number in my contacts. She rattled it off, and I called her so she'd have my number, too. "There. Now you can call me whenever."

"Cool."

I set my cell down and shook my towel out to get any dirt or bugs I might have been sitting on off before folding it up. The guys came back carrying all the floats. Benji flicked his in the air, spraying Becca and me with cold droplets of water. I laughed as I wiped myself dry.

"Want me to give you a ride to your place?" Alec asked after he tossed a few floats in the back of his truck.

"Nah, I'll just walk."

"You sure? I don't mind."

"It's not far. I'm good to walk." I'd walked here to begin with anyway. There was no point in having him drive me.

"You should let him give you a ride," Shane insisted. He was closer to me than I'd known. I hadn't heard him walk up. "Never know what might be waiting for you in those woods."

I swore something evil glistened in his eyes.

"Shut it," Becca said as she playfully slapped him on the back. "There's nothing in those woods during the day besides squirrels, rabbits, and possibly a deer or two."

"Never know," Shane muttered.

My stomach flip-flopped. Was there something in the woods? One of his brothers waiting for me maybe?

Even as anxiety prickled across my skin, I straightened my back and looked Shane square in the eye. There was no way I'd let him think he had frightened me. "Nothing has ever gotten me before."

"Always a first time for everything." He smirked.

I hated him. Once I found out where he was keeping Glenn and what the hell was going on with the abductions and money being paid situation, I was going to do bad things to him.

"I don't mind giving you a ride," Alec insisted, obviously feeling a need to insert himself into whatever was going on between Shane and me.

"I'm fine. I'll call you later." I stood on the tips of my toes and pecked Alec on the lips. When I broke the kiss and started to walk away, he grabbed my waist.

Alec spun me around until I faced him again and crushed his lips against mine. The slight brush of his tongue against my closed lips had my knees growing weak. His grip on me tightened as he pulled me closer. I melted against him. Something possessive about the kiss caught me off guard. Alec had always been sweet. I'd never seen this side of him before. I'd be lying if I said I didn't like it. It spoke to a piece of me Alec hadn't reached before. A piece that reminded me of Eli.

Guilt hit me, stinging my chest. How was it possible to be kissing Alec and thinking of Eli?

"Get a room," Benji grumbled as he smacked us on the head with one of the noodle floats.

We pulled apart. Alec chuckled while I tried to force away the sudden onslaught of guilt I felt building, but I found it difficult. Something inside of me was changing. I knew it had everything to do with the approaching full moon.

"Call me later," Alec said. "Or text, whatever."

"Okay."

"Have a good night." He leaned forward and brushed his lips against mine once more.

It made me wish we were alone. Never had I wanted to make out with him more than right now. The taste of him on my tongue, the feel of him pressed against me, had my insides tingling.

"You too." I licked my lips, tasting the remnants of him across them as I spun around to face the others. I waved pointedly to Becca and Benji, choosing to flat-out ignore Shane. He had to expect it. Everyone else did. I think it was becoming clear the two of us didn't get along. "See you guys later. Thanks for letting me hang out today. Oh, and call me sometime, Becca. Maybe we can do something together."

That got Shane's attention. I could feel his dark gaze on me. I guess he hadn't thought we'd gotten that close over the couple of times we'd hung out.

"I will, and remember what I said," Becca insisted. "Give

me a call tomorrow if you need any help with the twins. I love babies."

"I will. Thanks." I started toward the edge of the woods. Movement captured my attention and I felt my adrenaline spike. All I could think about was Shane's brothers. His fake concern about me walking home might have been a tip. One I'd foolishly ignored.

When Tate and Cooper stepped from the woods with fishing poles and tackle boxes in hand, I relaxed. How long had they been standing there? Had they been watching me the entire time? Did they see me kissing Alec?

"Good luck fishing," Shane shouted to the Vargas boys over the rumble of his truck. "Pretty sure we scared all the fish away for you." He revved his engine and sped away, kicking up bits of dirt and grass in the process.

Tate flipped him off. The sight of his middle finger high in the air made me laugh. It was totally something Eli would have done.

I slinked through the woods. Why was Eli all I could think about? We were just friends. Friends who dealt with pack business together. We also painted living room walls and ate macaroni. We drank moonshine, got each other, and had nearly kissed.

No.

Friends.

That was all we were, at least that was what I kept telling myself.

15

I woke Wednesday morning to the sound of Gran coaxing me to life.

"Tonight is the night," she whispered. "Time to rise and shine. We have a long day ahead of us."

I rubbed the sleep from my eyes, hoping the small movement would let her know I was awake so she'd leave me be. Five more minutes. That was all I wanted.

"Wakey, wakey," she said. This time, her voice sounded farther away. She was waking Gracie. She growled as she stretched. My sister was even less of a morning person than I was, which said a lot. "Up, lazybones. Now, you two," Gran said with more force. She clapped her hands together, startling my eyes open.

I forced myself to sit up in bed, relishing the bits of darkness that still cloaked the room. From previous experience, I knew if one of us didn't sit up and show true signs of waking, Gran would resort to flipping on the light switch, creating a strobe that blinded.

It was not something I wanted to deal with this morning. Today would be stressful enough.

"I'm up," I croaked. My voice sounded strange. I needed water. The tank top I'd worn to bed was dampened with sweat and stuck to my skin. I tossed my sheet off, but it didn't cool me enough. The room was too stuffy and hot.

"Good, breakfast will be ready in twenty minutes," Gran said from the doorway. The door made a soft click as she closed it behind her.

I wiped sweat from my brow. Hadn't I left the window open before drifting off to sleep? I thought I remembered propping the box fan in it too.

My gaze drifted to the window in question. It was closed and the fan sat on the floor, its blades not spinning. The sight of it irritated me. Who had closed it? Who'd turned the fan off? It was sweltering in here.

I narrowed my eyes on Gracie as I slipped out of bed. Soggy carpet squished beneath my feet. A slew of curse words spewed from my mouth. I tiptoed to the window and flung it open. Cool early morning air drifted into the room, making it easier to breathe, but it did nothing for the sopping mess on the floor. I reached for one of the dirty shirts Gracie had tossed on the floor and dried my feet.

"Why is the floor wet? And why did you close the window last night?" I growled at Gracie.

She sat up in bed and rubbed the sleep from her eyes. "It was raining, duh," Gracie snapped. "You put the stupid fan in the window and it kept blowing water in."

"It was hot last night. I was trying to cool it down in here. How was I supposed to know it was going to rain?"

"Whatever, you get to clean up the mess." She slipped out of bed and headed for the door.

I threw the dirty shirt I'd used to dry my feet at her, missing by a mile. She could aggravate the piss out of me sometimes. It was just like her to leave me to clean up the mess on my own.

I grabbed a couple of dirty towels out of my laundry basket and sopped up the water. What a great way to start my day. Had Gran noticed the water? She hadn't said anything. I hoped she never did. She was still upset about the last time it happened. The carpet was sure to have a funky mildew smell to it now.

Maybe it was time to ask again for an AC unit in our bedroom. There was one in the living room and Gran had one in her room, but we'd never had one in ours. We just suffered.

As soon as I finished sopping up the carpet, I propped the fan in the window again. It wasn't raining, so there shouldn't be an issue this time. It would circulate air through the room, help dry the carpet, and it would also help get rid of the moldy smell building.

I carried the towels I'd used to the bathroom and rang them out in the tub. The scent of bacon drifted to my nose, but I knew I wouldn't be able to eat any. It wasn't for me. Not today.

Today, I would only be able to eat fruits and vegetables.

Starving myself was part of the cleansing process everyone went through before a full moon ceremony. It was another thing I hated about these nights. While I didn't mind eating fruits and vegetables, I did enjoy meat. I knew some people could handle a vegetarian or vegan lifestyle, but I wasn't one of them. Maybe it had something to do with the werewolf genes in my DNA. Not eating animal protein left me crabby.

"Breakfast is ready," Gran shouted down the hall.

I draped the wet towels over the edge of the tub and dried my hands. "Coming."

My mouth watered as the scent of bacon intensified with each step I took toward the kitchen. My stomach grumbled painfully loud. I hoped Gran made something good for me this time. Last month, she'd given me a kale smoothie the color of dirt instead of the vibrant green I'd been expecting. It had tasted like grass, but she'd forced me to drink it anyway. I prayed for something better this morning.

The instant I stepped into the kitchen, I knew my prayers had been answered.

Apple slices of every color filled the bowl closest to me. Bowls of pineapple, every variety of melon, orange slices, grapes, strawberries, and pears were lined up beside it. A cluster of bananas sat beside a plate of kiwi cut into stars.

Gran had been busy this morning.

"Wow, this looks amazing," I insisted. It was so much better than the nasty smoothie she'd made last month.

"Thank you, dear." Gran smiled as she handed me a plate. It was the same fine china she pulled out every month when the moon was full.

Gran honored the moon goddess as much as possible. This was Gran's favorite time of the month. It always had been. Even before I was of age to drink the tea concoction meant to trigger a reaction and awaken the werewolf gene within me, I knew Gran loved the full moon. She claimed there was raw energy that was easy to tap. To her, it wasn't just about her wolf side; it was everything. She was a moon child through and through.

"I still feel bad for last month when I forced you to drink that horrible smoothie twice in one day and wanted to make it up to you. There's everything fruit you can think of, except for mangoes. I know they're your favorite, but they didn't look up to par. Not for today."

Gran had high standards when it came to the food we consumed today. Not just my food, but also everyone else's. The entire day was meant to be celebrated. You celebrated the moon, even if you weren't Moon Kissed. You were still a part of the pack.

I grabbed a few kiwi stars and a banana before moving down the lineup she'd created. Gracie stepped behind me and grabbed a plate from the stack set out. She bypassed the fruit and reached for a strip of bacon. I knew what she'd fill her plate with. It was always the same. Bacon, eggs, hash browns, and toast slathered with butter. She'd eat some fruit after I'd eaten my share. It was the way things went on mornings of the full moon.

"Where's Dad?" I asked. Either he'd passed out on the porch due to another drunken binge and Gran had left him there, or he'd never made it home.

"He'll be here. Don't you worry," Gran said with confidence as she stirred the scrambled eggs.

I wasn't worried. I figured he'd show up at some point. He always did.

"Hurry up and eat some fruit," Gracie demanded. "It looks good. I can't wait to get my hands on the honeydew."

"It's all yours," I whispered, hoping Gran wouldn't hear me. She'd forgotten, yet again, I didn't like honeydew. I didn't like cantaloupe either. Watermelon was the only melon I cared for.

The sound of a vehicle pulling up to our trailer made its way to my ears.

"There he is," Gran announced in a chipper voice.

Was she up to something? If so, it had to be something that involved my father.

"Oh, Mina, I forgot your drink." Gran swung open the fridge door and my heart sank. I'd foolishly thought because she'd felt bad about the kale smoothie last month I'd get away without having to taste another this month.

"What is it?" I asked as she stepped toward me carrying a glass with a milky liquid inside.

"Pure coconut water."

"Oh." I liked coconuts. While I'd never had coconut water before, it had to taste better than her smoothie.

The front door to our trailer opened and Dad stepped inside. I took in his appearance. He didn't seem as though he'd spent the night drinking. In fact, he looked clean-shaven and well rested. I also noticed his limp was virtually gone as he walked to where Gran stood.

"Looks like I'm just in time." He grinned before placing a kiss on her cheek.

"Grab a plate," Gran instructed.

"I will," Dad said. He shifted his attention to Gracie and me. "Mornin', girls. How are you feeling about tonight, Mina?"

"Okay, I guess," I said. I was so sick of being asked the same question each month.

"I have a feeling tonight will be the one," he said, same as every other morning of a full moon. "Which is why I went out and got you something." He pulled a narrow white box from his pant pocket and laid it on the table beside my plate.

"You didn't have to get me anything," I said, surprised.

"I know, but I wanted to. I have a feeling this is going to be it. You'll be Moon Kissed tonight. I wanted you to have something from me to commemorate it." He nodded toward the box. "Go on, open it. It's from Gran and me."

I glanced at Gran. A wide smile had stretched across her face. "I feel the same way your father does. The Moon Kiss will be upon you tonight. This moon feels different. There's so much energy to it. More than any other."

I wanted to tell them they might be wrong, but I bit my tongue. They both seemed so sure of themselves. I didn't want to be a downer, but I had my doubts.

Maybe I was wrong, though.

Gran had said this moon felt different. While I wasn't sure how it felt any different from the ones before, I'd learned early in life never to question one of her feelings.

"Go on, open it. They already said you could," Gracie insisted, her eyes glued to the box.

I reached for it. It was lighter in my hand than I'd anticipated. The hinges squeaked as I pried it open. Inside lay the most beautiful silver bracelet across a sheet of white satin. It was thick, but still delicate looking. The moon phases had been etched into its shiny surface.

"It's beautiful," I gushed. "Thank you." I stood to give them both a hug.

"You're welcome. I'm glad you like it," Dad said.

Gran pulled me into her arms. "You're going to need it after tonight. I can feel it. There's some serious energy coursing through the air with this moon. I'm telling you."

Hope blossomed through my chest. Maybe this bracelet would be my good luck charm. Maybe it would draw the moon goddess's attention to me so she'd allow me to become Moon Kissed.

Silver helped keep us connected to the moon. It helped to keep our wolf on a leash, to maintain control over our wolf self throughout the month, and also to allow us to change when we wanted. Not just on a full moon. Once a person became Moon Kissed, they needed to wear silver. If they didn't, and the connection with the moon was ever to become severed, I wasn't sure what would happen but I knew it wouldn't be good.

"It's pretty," Gracie said, pulling my thoughts back to the bracelet. "Can I see it?"

I passed the box to her, still unbelieving they had gotten me anything. Tonight's full moon seemed to hold a lot of weight before the gift, but now it had doubled. I didn't understand why. It wasn't as though this was the last full moon of my eighteenth year. Everyone sure was acting as if it were, though.

"I love it," Gracie said as she continued to stare at the bracelet. Her fingertips grazed the smooth surface, touching each of the engraved moon symbols. "It looks familiar."

The second she said the words, I felt the same way. I had seen it before. I couldn't remember where though. Maybe not this exact one, but I remembered the engravings of the moon phases on a piece of jewelry.

"I gave your mother something similar when we first started dating," Dad said. His voice was low and pained. "It wasn't a bracelet; it was a necklace with a long pendant charm on it that had the same moon phases engraved."

An image of it flashed through my mind. I could see my mom leaning over to give me a goodnight kiss and the pendant charm touching my face. "I remember that. She never took it off."

"No, she didn't." Dad chuckled as though struck by a memory himself. "The one time she did, you nearly lost it. We found it in Gran's garden two days later."

"Oh! I'd forgotten all about that! I wanted that necklace so bad. I'd put it on in the bathroom, but then Gran called me out to the garden and I couldn't get it off. I didn't want to break it or tell anyone I'd put it on, so I left it. Then I forgot about it. I don't know how, but it managed to fall off when I was helping her. Gosh, I remember Mom being so upset while she searched for it."

"I remember too. It was mixed in with my lavender," Gran said. "That used to be your favorite to harvest."

"It still is." Not because it smelled good, but because there were so many uses for it. If I had retained anything from Gran at all, it was that lavender was good for just about any ailment.

Gracie took the bracelet out of its box and held it out to me. "Can I put it on you?"

I flashed her a smile and nodded. Our morning mishap over the soaked bedroom floor had been forgotten. "Sure."

She wrapped the bracelet around my wrist and her tiny fingers fumbled with the clasp. "There," she said once it was secured in place. "It looks good on you. Plus, I like that it reminds me of Mom."

I made a mental note to get her one similar when the time came. "Yeah, me too."

"It does look beautiful on you," Gran insisted. "But I

think it's time you focus on eating breakfast. You know how important it is to purify your system and fill yourself with as many nutrients as possible. It makes the first shift easier on your body."

I reached for one of the kiwi stars. My gaze drifted back to the bracelet. Another image of Mom wearing her necklace floated through my mind. God, I missed her. I wished she were here.

Why had she left us?

I knew why. She couldn't handle Dad's addiction to pain pills or alcohol. Didn't she stop to think her leaving would only make those issues worse?

"There's still so much to do in order to prepare for tonight," Gran insisted, pulling me from my thoughts.

She was right. I picked up another piece of kiwi. It was time I prepared my body in case everyone was right and tonight ended up being the night I became Moon Kissed.

16

I reached for another cheesecloth baggie and scooped three teaspoons of the mushy herb paste inside. The salvia leaves had been harvested from Gran's garden, dried in our pantry, and then added to a large mason jar where they were covered with water and set in a patch of bright moonlight overnight to become a lunar infusion.

The musky, earthy scent I'd grown to detest wafted to my nose in the process of scooping the herbs into the cheesecloth baggie. I handed it off to Gracie next. She folded the opening closed, added a long piece of string, and stapled it shut before passing it to Gran. She wrapped it in wax paper and tucked it in a silver drawstring sachet. This was our process. Every month the three of us sat down and created the assembly line that would make enough tea bags for those who were of age to become Moon Kissed in the trailer park.

This month there were five of us. Tate Vargas, Millie Hess, Davey Hess, Violet Marshall, and me. It was Violet's first time drinking the tea. She'd just come of age on the eleventh of the month. I felt for her. It was never easy getting past the first taste of salvia tea. I remembered asking Gran once why she didn't add peppermint or honey to tone down the bitterness. She'd told me it would dilute the potency of the salvia, which was something she wouldn't dream of doing.

Honestly, nothing anyone said could prepare Violet for the horrible taste she was about to experience. While the measuring of the tea was precise each time, the taste was different. Sometimes it was stronger; others it wasn't.

"And that's that," Gran said once she'd tucked the final tea sack into one of her sachets. She placed them in a ziplock bag and passed them to Gracie. "Try not to dawdle at the Vargases."

Gracie's cheeks tinted pink. "I won't."

I guess I wasn't the only one who'd noticed she had a boyfriend. Gran seemed to have picked up on it too. Figured. Gran always seemed to notice everything.

Gracie opened the front door and stepped out onto the porch. The sound of the weed eater blasted through the trailer along with the scent of freshly cut grass. This was the one time of the month Dad stayed sober enough to do stuff around the place. Whatever he did next, it would definitely be outdoors. When the full moon came around, his back always felt better than ever, and you could find him outside doing something useful.

I wondered if I could talk him into doing some repairs on my car.

"Okay, it's time for you to eat some vegetables now," Gran insisted the second Gracie was out the front door. She got up from the dining room table with more speed than usual. Normally, her old joints and bones popped and rebelled against sudden movement, but not today. It was the magic of the full moon. "You have a choice: cucumbers and tomatoes, or sliced bell peppers and radishes?"

I wasn't a big fan of radishes. They were spicy and never failed to give me a stomachache. "I'll take cucumbers and tomatoes, please. Can I have a little salt with them?"

"Just a smidgen of Himalayan sea salt. Nothing more."

I cleaned up the mess we'd made while making the sachets as Gran prepared my afternoon snack. That was one of the perks to this day. Gran cooked for me and prepared all my snacks. I didn't have to lift a finger.

By the time I finished washing the tools we'd used and wiping off the table, Gran had an entire plate of sliced cucumbers and tomatoes waiting on me. She handed me a plain glass of ice water this time, and I gladly accepted. Coconut water hadn't been my thing. I didn't care how amazing the benefits of drinking it were, plain coconut water tasted gross.

"I need to finish preparing your garments for tonight," Gran said as she disappeared down the hall. "Time is running out, and I feel like I still have so much to do before nightfall."

"Do you want any help?" I called after her, even though I knew her answer would be no.

She never wanted help. Not when it came to this. She preferred to do it all on her own.

"Absolutely not, you know you're supposed to rest and relax."

"In that case, I think I'll head to the lake for a while. Clear my head. Prepare." While stressing over the details of the ceremony and preparing everything was Gran's ritual each full moon, mine was a quiet walk to the lake where I sat for a while enjoying nature.

"Go right ahead," Gran replied. "Make sure you're back by dinner, though. You still have one more meal of veggies before you drink the tea."

"I'll be back before then," I promised as I headed for the door.

Dad was refilling his weed eater string when I stepped out onto the porch. Sweat beaded across his brow.

"Off to take your usual stroll around the lake?" he asked as he smacked the spindle of string into place with the palm of his hand.

"Yeah, I'll be back later. If I don't leave now, Gran is going to stuff me full of more veggies or fruit. I can't handle anymore fruit."

"I'm sure." Dad chuckled. "Just remember to be back before dinner, or she'll really be on your case."

I started down the stairs and headed toward the lake. "I know."

Hot air rolled over me as a gust of wind blew. The sweltering sun beat down against my bare shoulders, warming my skin as I walked toward the woods. A dip in the lake would feel good.

"Hey there, Mina," the Bell sisters said in unison as I reached their trailer. They were on their porch, as usual, fanning themselves with gigantic paper fans. Tall glasses of lemonade decorated with tiny pink umbrellas sat on a table between them.

"Hi," I said with a wave.

"You ready for tonight?" the older of the two sisters asked.

"I guess." I shrugged, not knowing what else to say.

"Did you get a little something to commemorate this one?" the youngest sister asked, nodding to my bracelet.

Nothing got by them, did it? They were worse than Gran.

I held my wrist out so they could see my bracelet. "I did. It was a gift from Gran and my dad."

"Looks like quite a few people in your life have high hopes this will be the moon for you," she said as she arched one of her drawn-on brows.

"Yeah, they do." I crammed my hands into the back pockets of my shorts, wishing this conversation would end. All I wanted to do was head to the lake.

"I don't blame them. This one feels important, doesn't it? I think it's going to be the biggest strawberry moon we've seen in years," the oldest of the sisters said.

They could feel it too? Someone always claimed each moon held a greater energy than the last, but I'd never heard so many agree about it at once. Something was different about this one. Something bigger. Everyone seemed to notice.

My attention drifted around the trailer park. Everyone seemed to be out and about. Kids were running around playing. Some people were tending to their yards while others grilled food. The entire park was alive and buzzing with excitement.

"Mina, hey! You coming or what?" Eli shouted from the edge of the woods. He'd startled me, but I knew what he was doing and I was grateful.

He was saving me from the Bell sisters.

"Yeah," I yelled back and waved to him. "Just a sec."

"Oh, I see the oldest Vargas boy is waiting on you," one of

the Bell sisters said. "He sure is a cute little thing. Best not keep him waiting. Run along now."

"Uh, thanks. Have a good rest of your day," I said as I started toward Eli.

"Good luck tonight, Mina. We're rooting for you," the oldest of the sisters called after me.

"Thank you!" I shouted over my shoulder.

I cruised past Mr. Russel's trailer. The game show he was watching blasted through his open windows and out onto the gravel road where I walked. It was ironic how he always made the most noise throughout the day, but come nightfall, he wanted utter silence.

"Looked like you were caught in the Bell sisters' web back there." Eli grinned as we started through the woods together.

"I was. You know how those two can be. They can talk for hours."

"Oh, I know." He nodded. "Which was why I decided to be nice and save you. Figured you'd be heading to the lake today. You always do."

"You've got me all figured out, don't you?" I glanced at him. His skin had darkened since the last time I'd seen him. It made the color of his eyes pop even more. He must've been working outside again this week.

"I know you're guaranteed to pay the lake at least one visit on the day of a full moon."

I was predictable like that; there was no denying it. The lake was my place. It was where I could decompress. Where I could think.

"Then you know I don't prefer company," I said.

"I know, but I had to make it believable for the sisters.

You know they were watching to see if we'd go into the woods together."

I almost wished he'd said something different—like maybe ask me if I wanted company this one time. When he didn't, I deflated.

"I'll catch up with you later," he said before veering off in another direction.

"Oh, okay." I tried to keep my disappointment from entering my voice.

"Good luck tonight," Eli said before he disappeared into a thick patch of woods.

"Thanks," I whispered even though he was already gone.

I continued toward the lake, struggling to push thoughts of Eli from my mind. The second I stepped into the clearing of the lake, all thoughts vanished. Nothing existed besides the beautiful scenery and me. Nature. It was exactly where I needed to be.

It was an integral part of my purification process before each full moon.

I positioned myself at the edge of the water on my favorite stump. I wasn't sure when the tree had been cut down or why, but its remnants made for an excellent seat. With my legs folded, I placed my hands on my knees, palms facing up. For a moment, all I did was soak in the scenery and feel the warm sunshine touching my skin. The lake was quiet. No one seemed to be swimming, boating, or fishing in its waters. It was my lucky day.

My mind wandered from thoughts of Eli, to the moon, to my bracelet, and finally to my mom. She had told me once that coming to the lake on the day of a full moon had been something she always did to clear her head beforehand. It was where I'd gotten the idea from, but not my love for the lake. That was my own. So was meditation.

While my mom had said she came to the lake and sat, watching nature and the few people mingling about, I came to meditate. It wasn't something I did on a regular basis, though, only during a full moon. It calmed my frazzled mind. Made me forget how nervous I was about the events of the night—about what might happen, or what might never.

Mom had never had to worry. She was Moon Kissed during the full moon right after her seventeenth birthday. Dad had been even luckier. He'd found out on his third time of drinking the salvia tea.

Gran was right. I was a late bloomer. That had to be it.

My gaze drifted to the silver bracelet on my wrist. It had become heavy, weighted down with the worry I might not need it, not in the way it had been intended. I'd always thought I would be okay if I never became Moon Kissed. I thought if Sylvie Hess could hack it so could I, but now I wasn't so sure. I didn't want to be a non-shifting member of the pack. I didn't want to be different for the rest of my life. I'd spent enough time being different. I was ready to step out of the weird limbo place I'd been since birth. I wanted to be like my family. I wanted to be like my pack, minus Sylvie.

I wanted to be Moon Kissed.

A gust of wind blew, wafting the scent of hot lake water in my face. I closed my eyes and exhaled a slow breath. For the next few minutes, I focused on the start and stop of each breath. My body relaxed as my breathing evened out. My mind wandered to the ceremony as thoughts of the tea not triggering my wolf gene surfaced, but I let them float away and circled back to my breathing. That was what meditation was about. Focusing on your natural breath. Not keeping your mind clear of all thought. Thoughts would happen. It was how you reacted to them in the moment that mattered.

Time seemed to stand still as I allowed myself a few minutes. This was my timeout for the night. It was when I'd allow any stress or anxiety to melt away.

A twig snapped somewhere behind me, and the fine hairs on the back of my neck stood on end. I fought with the desire to glance back and see what or who it was. A prickly sensation built across my skin. Was I being watched? Leaves rustled from a few feet away, but I could feel no wind. My eyes snapped open. Chills crept along my spine as adrenaline flooded my system.

Someone was behind me.

I could feel their gaze on me. Seconds passed before I was able to make myself glance over my shoulder. At first, I didn't see anything, but then movement in a thicket caught my attention. Someone wearing a navy-blue shirt was walking away from me. I couldn't see his hair color due to the thickness of the woods he was concealed by, but I could judge how tall he was and how muscular, and that, whoever he was, he was definitely male.

My heart palpitated in my throat. Was it Shane? One of his brothers maybe? Or could it be one of the Vargas boys checking up on me again? Eli maybe? I tried to remember what color shirt he'd been wearing, but couldn't. Eli wouldn't have stood there staring at me, though.

I forced myself to stand, dusted my bottom off, and started back to the trailer park. Sitting out here alone might not have been the best idea, even in daylight. Just because I wasn't Moon Kissed didn't mean I was safe. Shane and his brothers suspected I was a wolf because of where I lived. That might be all the reason they needed to abduct me.

Yeah, I was a sitting duck if I stayed out here.

I quickened my pace in a hurry to get back to the others. When I cut through the brambles that blocked the trailer park, all the tension I'd been harboring left my body. Safety washed over me. For the moment, at least.

17

"Here," Gracie said as she slipped into the bathroom. I was in the tub, bathing myself in the sweet scented milky concoction Gran created for me every full moon. "Gran told me to bring you this plate. She wants you to finish eating this, because if not, it's going to go bad in the fridge." She set a plate with sliced cucumber on the edge of the bathtub.

"Thanks." I sighed as I picked up a slice and bit into it. I was over vegetables. I was over fruit. All I wanted was meat. Bread would even be a nice addition.

"Are you nervous?" Gracie asked the same question every month, but this time there was more weight packed behind it.

"Not really," I lied, popping the entire cucumber slice in my mouth. Of course I was nervous. I was surprised she couldn't see my hands shaking.

"I would be. I mean, you only have a couple of full moons left." Her gaze drifted from me to her fingers. She picked at her cuticles. "What if you don't become Moon Kissed?"

"I don't know." It was an honest an answer. "Life will go on, I guess."

"Not the way it should."

"Says who?"

"Cooper," she whispered. "He says if you don't, then you won't be a member of the pack. Not really. You'd be an outsider. Someone with a glimpse inside, but nothing more."

Damn Cooper for getting her all worked up.

"I'll be fine," I insisted, hoping to reassure her. "Sylvie Hess is fine."

"I guess." She fidgeted where she stood. "Don't you want to be Moon Kissed?"

"Of course," I scoffed.

"Then why are you acting like it doesn't matter?"

I said the first thing that came to mind. "How I feel is the only the thing I can control."

Silence built between us. I reached out for another cucumber slice and bit into it. Gracie continued to pick at her cuticles without looking at me.

"I think I'll light a candle and say a prayer to the moon goddess for you," Gracie said in a soft voice.

"Thank you."

She headed for the door but paused before opening it. "I think your time is almost up. Gran should be in soon with your dress."

My fingertips looked like prunes. "You're probably right."

I didn't mind the cleansing bath. It was the best part of the whole purifying process. The herbs didn't smell horrible, and the water made my skin silky smooth.

A few minutes after Gracie left, a soft knock sounded at the door.

"Mina, time's up," Gran called through the thin door before she opened it. Draped over her arm was the white dress I was supposed to wear. She hung it on a hook behind the door and shifted to face me. There was a wide smile stretched across her face. "This is going to be it. I can feel it," she said as she clasped her hands together beneath her chin, her smile growing. She reminded me of a child excited by the prospect of something fantastic and wonderful occurring.

"I hope so," I muttered before I could stop myself.

"It will happen, child," Gran said as she reached for the knob. Had my doubt killed her confidence in the situation, or was she upset with me for being so negative? "Change into the dress. Then we can be on our way."

A shiver slipped through me, and I pulled my knees to my chest. The full moon ceremony was nearly upon me.

I pulled the plug once Gran left the room and climbed out of the tub. My fingers reached for the soft, fluffy towel I'd set on the toilet seat before getting in. It was one reserved for full moons only.

After I dried off, I pulled the sheer white dress from the hook on the door. The fabric was still slightly warm from Gran ironing it. This was another good part of the ceremony —dressing up. I was more of a jeans and T-shirt kind of girl, but enjoyed getting dressed up once in a while. I slipped the soft fabric over my head and let it cascade down my body, falling to just above my ankles. The first time I wore it floated through my mind. Gran had to hem it because it pooled around my feet so much. A couple times a year, she let the hem out as I grew. A few months ago, she'd released it for the final time. There was no more fabric to be let out. No more

191

length to be added. It was what it was, and I was about to completely outgrow it.

The time to be Moon Kissed was now, if ever.

———

TWIGS SNAPPED beneath my feet as I walked with the others to our secret place in the woods reserved for moon ceremonies and pack runs. Gran led us like always. She was the eldest of the pack. Although, if you stood her beside the Bell sisters, you wouldn't be able to tell. Gran looked much younger than they did, even though she wasn't. She had almost a decade on the oldest Bell sister.

Tree branches scraped across my skin as I continued along the path behind the others. Each of us hoped to be Moon Kissed tonight. Would it happen?

"I think I'm going to be sick," Violet said from the front of the line. My heart went out to her.

"You'll be fine," Davey said from behind her. His voice was calm and gentle, but I could hear a slight quiver when he spoke. His mental state wasn't any better than hers. It was sweet of him to offer her comfort, though.

"Shh, no speaking children," Gran hissed. We were close to the ritual grounds, but not there yet. Gran thought it was respectful to enter the place in utter silence, so had the elders before her.

It was a mystical place. Tucked into a mountain near the lake, it was one of the most beautiful places in Mirror Lake. A hidden gem. You could see the water, but there was also a cave and plenty of woods to marvel at as well. The best part was, it was ours. No one else knew it was here. At least not any humans. Besides the members of the pack, there were a few witches living in Mirror Lake who knew it existed, but only because they had created the spell that kept the place a secret.

We offered them protection, and in return, they kept the spell that hid our monthly rituals and sacred place up.

"Take your seats, children," Gran instructed the five of us once we reached the clearing.

We did as we were told. My hair floated around my face as a gentle breeze kicked up, and I rested my hands in my lap, waiting for Gran to pass me my tea. I wanted to get this over with. The not knowing if everyone was right about this moon was eating at me. My heart thundered in my chest as my hands grew clammy.

I glanced out at the pack as they stood watching the five of us settle into a comfortable seated position. Gracie looked as nervous as I felt, but Dad seemed to buzz with excitement. When Eli stepped forward to start the ritual fire, I struggled to remember when his father had passed the responsibility to him. He lit it the last few months, I knew that much, but I couldn't remember the first.

Gran crossed in front of me, heading to the lake with a silver bucket in her arms. She dipped it in the water and filled it halfway, taking only the water that resided in the reflection of the moon. I didn't know much about the process, but I knew that was important. We were supposed to take a piece of the moon inside us during this ceremony. It was a way to allow the moon goddess a glimpse at our soul. She was supposed to use it to determine if we were ready to become Moon Kissed, to be given a wolf.

I imagined there wasn't an inch of my soul the moon

goddess hadn't glimpsed by now. What more would she need to see in order to allow me to become Moon Kissed?

Gran carried the bucket to the fire Eli had started and poured the water into a black kettle waiting. Gracie then went to each of the families of those sitting beside me and gathered the sachets she'd given them the previous day. Their intentions for their loved one would be embedded within the leaves of the tea by now.

Thick smoke billowed into the air, drawing my attention back to Gran. She'd touched the tips of a bundle of dried herbs to the fire. This wasn't unusual. I'd seen it a million times. In fact, I knew what would happen next—Gran would ward away negative energy that might have congregated in this area since the last full moon. She'd also circle each of us waiting to drink the tea as another form of purification. Still, the sweet familiar scent of the herbs induced panic inside me as it floated to my nose. I closed my eyes as Gran circled me first with smoke. My mind slipped away as I focused on my breath and forced myself to relax, tapping into my meditation skills.

Gracie slipped a small teacup into my hands, and I knew the moment of judgment was upon me. The sharp scent of heated salvia tickled my nose as steam rose from the mug. I kept my eyes closed tight, knowing from experience it was for the best. If I glanced at the faces of the pack while I drank, my anxiety would come rushing back full force and make keeping the tea down that much harder.

A tiny bell chimed—the signal to drink.

I placed the mug to my lips and tried not to shiver with disgust when the first droplets of tea touched my tongue. God, it was so bitter. Potent. Horrible. Exactly as I'd remembered. My stomach churned as I continued to down the nastiness. When I was finished, I held my breath, keeping my eyes closed, and waited.

Nothing happened. Maybe nothing ever would.

My skin tingled as I felt my face redden. The breath I'd been holding came out with a whoosh as pinpricks of ice shot through my chest.

I was never going to be Moon Kissed.

The moon goddess didn't think I was worthy. She didn't want me to be a part of my pack. She wanted me to be like Sylvie Hess. An outsider forever.

I opened my eyes and saw the faces of the others staring at me expectedly. If I knew how to fake this—if it were possible—I'd do it so I wouldn't have to see the disappointment dull their happiness when they learned another moon had passed and Mina Ryan hadn't walked away Moon Kissed again.

What would they say once they were back home, exhausted from their run, preparing for bed? Would they pity me, or would they talk about how they knew it would never happen for me? That this time would be no different from the others.

My gaze drifted across each of their faces. No one seemed to be looking at me specifically except for my family. Worry creased Gracie's forehead, but Gran and Dad looked high on anticipation. I couldn't look at them. I couldn't look at any of them. At least that's what I thought until my gaze settled on Eli.

His stare was intense, but I somehow found it calming. He didn't show any sense of anticipation as he watched me. The ghost of a smile quirked at the corners of his mouth as we continued staring at one another. It caused butterflies to break into flight in the pit of my stomach, and my cheeks to heat for a different reason.

How was it possible Eli Vargas could elicit such feelings from me in a time like this?

18

I lost track of how much time had passed since I'd finished my tea. Seconds? Minutes? Hours? Time seemed to drag on without any meaning attached to it once the tea had been consumed. Sweat beaded across my brow. I wasn't sure if it was because of the warm temperature or something else. My dress began to stick to me in places, and my heart picked up its rhythm. When the faces of the pack members swirled, melting together with the fire, I knew something was happening. Something that involved the tea.

Was this it? Was this what it felt like when the moon goddess chose you?

My vision darkened around the edges as the world seemed to tip on its axis. The ground in front of me rippled, bubbling with movement that shouldn't be there. Nausea built in my stomach, causing bile to rise up the back of my throat. My ears hummed with the sounds of the night, everything suddenly amplified. I swallowed hard, fighting the urge to vomit.

White light above me caught my eye. I lifted my gaze to the star-speckled sky. The moon looked larger than normal and its otherworldly glow ten times brighter. Was it falling? Alarm nipped at my insides, chilling the blood flowing through my veins.

Child of the Moon, a soft voice called.

It wasn't mine, but the words were inside my head. Sweat slickened my skin. My breathing hitched. What was happening to me?

Open up to me. Do not fear. Do not resist. Let me bless you...

How did I do any of those things? Why would I want to?

The dress I wore became saturated with sweat. Why was I so hot? The temperature of the air didn't feel hot. Did I have a fever? Was something wrong with me? My stomach rolled as my mouth pooled with saliva.

Oh, God. I was going to hurl.

My hand came to my mouth, but in slow motion. The realization jarred me. Why couldn't I move correctly? I waved my hand in front of my face. A trippy trail followed behind it. Had Gran given me a bad batch? Had I drunk too much?

This couldn't be right. Something had to be wrong. No one had ever described the process to be like this.

I shifted to glance at the others beside me. They'd drank the tea, too. If I were having a reaction because the tea was bad, they would be as well.

It didn't take long to notice they all seemed to be having the same reaction I was.

Sweat beaded across their skin, circles rimmed their eyes, and they each appeared to be as out of it as I felt. A small sense of calm settled over me. At least I wasn't the only one. I closed my eyes. My teeth chattered as my body temperature went from fiery hot to freezing cold in the span of a single heartbeat. The contrast startled my eyes open. I opened my mouth to say something, but the faces of the pack members blurred together until they became one screwed up face. A scream built in the back of my throat, but it died when everyone seemed to drift away.

Suddenly I was alone.

This couldn't be right. People couldn't vanish into thin air. Not the wolves from my pack. Witches, maybe. I blinked, thinking my eyes had to be playing tricks on me. Still no pack. No Gran. No Dad. No Gracie. No one.

Where had everyone disappeared to?

I was alone with a fire crackling a few feet away. The woods still sounded with nighttime creatures as I held my breath and listened. Nothing about the space had changed. Except for the lake. A heavy fog had moved in at some point, giving the rippling dark waters an ominous vibe.

What was I supposed to do? Sit here and wait? For what, I didn't know.

I closed my eyes and pulled in a deep breath, thinking maybe when I opened them things would go back to the way they'd been. After counting to five, I opened my eyes to find I was still alone.

I stood and glanced around. Maybe I hadn't been able to gauge time because of the tea. Could it be everyone had already gone out on a run or went home? I took a step toward the woods and witnessed the trees grow thirty feet in height within the span on a single step. Their branches moved in an unfelt breeze that intensified when I took another step forward. Leaves and debris blew, tangling in my hair and forcing me to shield my eyes. I took a step back and the wind died down.

Okay. Apparently, I'd stepped in the wrong direction. Also, this place wasn't normal. It wasn't our typical ritual spot and that wasn't my lake.

Still, I needed to decide what to do next, because standing here wasn't an option. I chewed my bottom lip as I contemplated between walking toward the cave or the lake.

I went toward the lake.

The reflection of the moon shimmered across its surface. Maybe it was a sign I was supposed to go toward it. My heart thundered as I forced myself to inch toward it, my gaze locked on its smooth waters. Instantly, the smooth waters rippled. At first, I thought it was in an effort to draw the reflection of the moon closer to me, but as I took another step forward, the ripples doubled in size and doubt crept in.

I froze when massive waves that held the power to wipe out an entire city built before me. They pounded against one another at the edge of the lake, building until they formed a gigantic wall of water that seemed to beg me to take another step toward it. My beautiful lake wanted to wash me away. I stepped back. The wall of water receded. In seconds, all was as it was moments before.

My hands reached to tuck my hair behind my ears as a tremble slipped through me. I didn't know what was going on, but I did know all was left was the cave.

What would I do if something happened when I stepped toward it, too? My gaze drifted in a circle around me. Had I missed anything? Was I supposed to leave this space, or remain where I was? My rapid heartbeats counted out the seconds as they passed. The noises of the forest grew louder. The moon too bright. I couldn't stay here.

The cave was my only other option.

I pulled in a deep breath and started toward it on wobbly knees. Nothing happened. No bats the size of my head came out like I'd imagined. No bear ten times the size it should be growled in my face. Nothing. Maybe this was the way I was supposed to go, after all.

I continued forward until I was swallowed by the darkness resting inside. My fingers trailed along the cave's cool, bumpy walls as I made my way deeper in. The air grew stale and musky, but I pressed forward one foot in front of the other. When the walls became narrow, panic pumped through my system. Tight spaces had never bothered me before, but this place didn't feel normal. Thoughts of being trapped intensified what I was feeling. My feet faltered when my anxiety crested, and I closed my eyes to gather myself. I didn't know where I was going, but knew it was the only way I could go. The only way this place, whatever it was, would allow.

Something brushed against my back, causing me to jump. It was hard, rigid, cool to the touch, and tall. I froze. When it pressed against me harder, touching me from head to toe, I nearly lost it. I wanted to step forward, to run, to scream, but I couldn't. Fear had frozen me in place. My fingertips drifted behind me to feel what my eyes couldn't see in the darkness. Something solid. Something like rock.

No, no, no!

My breath burst in and out of my chest as I felt along a wall of smooth stone behind me. How was it possible a wall was behind me? My mind glitched, jumping to my next thought before the first had enough time to marinade.

I was trapped.

A whimper escaped my parted lips. It echoed against the rocks. Tears built in my eyes, but I refused to let them fall. I refused to break down.

After all, it could be a dream.

Placing one foot in front of the other, I continued forward, choosing to hold on to the notion this was all a dream even if it wasn't. Time passed and a light captured my attention in the distance. The sight of it propelled my feet forward faster. Woods lit by moonlight became visible as an exit to the cave emerged. I didn't care what waited for me beyond the stone walls; all I wanted was to be free from the cave's confines.

When I stumbled from the cave, I realized I was back where I started. The ritual space. Again, I was alone. Nothing had changed. It was as though I'd walked in a full circle somehow. Tears of frustration built, but again, I refused to let them fall. They wouldn't help me any.

Movement from the corner of my eye captured my attention.

A wolf at the edge of the woods where they met with the lake sat staring at me. Something about its presence was calming and familiar. I couldn't look away. It was a shade of brown that shimmered in the light of the moon. I stood still, worried any movement would startle it away. I didn't want to be alone again. Not in this place.

All I could do was stare.

Something about the wolf called to me. Its gaze drifted from me to the moon. I expected its jaws to open and for a beautifully terrifying howl to spill free, but it remained silent. Our eyes locked, and I found myself creeping toward it as if pulled by an unseen magnetic force. The wolf didn't move. Its gaze remained fixated on mine. This close I could make out the color of its eyes. Hazel. The same shade as mine.

When the wolf bowed its head as though answering my thought, something shifted inside me. A strange sense of knowing filled my every fiber. I knew this wolf. She was mine.

My hand reached out to touch her, wondering what her fur would feel like between my fingers. Her gaze never wavered. Fear didn't register from her, only interest. I held my breath as my fingertips inched closer to her. The instant I brushed against her soft fur, a blinding white light became all I could see. It stemmed from nowhere and everywhere at once, encompassing me.

United as one, so mote it be, the soft voice from before said as it floated through my mind.

I wasn't afraid hearing it this time, because I understood what was happening.

The moon goddess had kissed us both, and now we were one.

The blinding white light faded away. As did the feel of soft fur against my fingertips. My eyes fluttered open as my heart skipped a beat.

I was back with my pack.

The wolf was gone. A small sense of sadness trickled through me even though I was back where I should be. Something nudged my insides. It was warm and wild. Gentle and free.

My wolf.

A sense of wholeness filled me. She was still with me. I'd become one with her. I could feel her. She was an integral part of me now, same as I was to her.

My breath stilled in my chest as I focused on her. How had I ever felt complete without her?

Movement from my pack members in front of me captured my attention. I needed to find Gran. She would be so happy to know I'd been Moon Kissed, to know she was right. Something different had been in the air this moon. Dad and Gracie would be ecstatic for me, too.

Where was Gran? And what was wrong with my eyes?

Something about my view was off. Everyone was taller than I remembered. Or was I slouching? Whispers buzzed around me, but I couldn't focus on what was being said. No. That wasn't it. I could focus; I just didn't understand. Their words made no sense to me. It was as though they were speaking in a new language.

Had something in my brain broken during the process of becoming Moon Kissed?

Movement to my left caught my eye. A dark-haired wolf paced beside me. A sense of familiarity hummed through my system as I stared at the creature, but I didn't understand it. This wasn't my wolf. She was a different color. When I peeked around her, I spotted three wolves.

Oh my God, everyone who drank the tea had become a wolf. Did that mean? Was I?

I glanced down at myself. Brown fur glimmered in the moonlight instead of the white dress I'd been wearing.

I was my wolf. She was me.

The air around me charged with electricity, drawing my attention away from myself. I knew what was happening instantly—the others were changing. I could feel their presence transforming into something more relatable to my current form.

A wolf with soft gray hair that was nearly white stepped to my side. *Gran.* Not only could I feel her presence inside the wolf, I could smell her familiar scent lingering on her fur. She nuzzled against me, and I closed my eyes before burrowing my head into her fur. Warmth and happiness enveloped me. I felt like I'd come home, like I finally belonged.

Gran nuzzled into me one final time before disappearing into the thicket of woods behind us along with the others and our alpha. Those who weren't of age to be Moon Kissed began being led back to the park by Sylvie.

Maybe she did have a place in the pack after all.

A dark brown wolf larger than me caught my eye. He stood at the edge of the woods, watching me with a set of intensely green eyes I knew well. Amusement shimmered through them as Eli nodded toward the woods.

I started toward him on my new legs, feeling the solid ground beneath me bring a sense of stability and strength. I was connected to nature in a way I had never been before as I made my way toward him. It was magnificent. The second I reached Eli, he broke into a run. I wasn't sure if he wanted me to chase him, or if he was in a hurry to catch up with the others. It didn't matter. In three strides, I was at his side. Seconds later, I was taking part in my first moonlit pack run, and it was glorious.

19

My body ached as I rolled over in bed. For a moment, I'd forgotten why I was so sore, but then the events of the night came rushing back. A smirked twisted my lips. All the pain I was feeling was worth it.

"How was it?" Gracie whispered. She was lying in her bed, staring at me, as though she'd been waiting for me to wake.

"Amazing." There was no other word to describe it.

"Did it hurt? The shifting part?"

I thought for a moment, trying to remember. "No, it really didn't."

"Then all the stories everyone tells are bogus?" There was relief reflected in her words.

"Yeah."

Gracie propped her head up with the palm of her hand. "How are you feeling today?"

I yawned and stretched my arms above my head as I sat up in bed. "Sore, tired, exhilarated..."

"Well, congratulations." She smiled. "I was beginning to wonder if you were ever going to be Moon Kissed," she teased.

"You and me both." I laughed. "And probably every member of the pack." I flipped my blankets off and stood. I couldn't lay in bed any longer, not even to talk to Gracie. My body needed to move. A buzzing of excitement coursed through me that was hard to ignore.

The scent of bacon met my nose the instant I stepped into the hall. My stomach grumbled as I started toward the kitchen.

"Wow, shifting must make you work up a hefty appetite." Gracie giggled from behind me. "That sounded like it hurt."

I pushed on my stomach. "It sort of did. I'm starved."

Gran flashed me a wide smile as I entered the kitchen. "There you are. Oh, Mina, I'm so proud of you," she insisted as unshed tears glimmered in her eyes. "You adjusted so well last night to your new form. Congratulations on becoming Moon Kissed, honey. I knew you would. I had a gut feeling it would happen."

"Thanks." I moved to give her a hug and inspect what she was cooking. Bacon, eggs, hash browns, pancakes, biscuits, and gravy. "Wow. You're cooking every breakfast food there is."

"When something in life occurs that's worthy of celebrating, the only way to do it is with food."

I grabbed a piece of bacon and took a bite. "I can't argue with that. I'm starved this morning."

"Where's your bracelet?" She nodded to my bare wrist.

Where was my bracelet? "I think it's in my room somewhere."

"Make sure you wear silver each day. You have to keep a leash on your wolf."

Already I'd forgotten one of the most vital rules of being Moon Kissed. Seemed as though I was off to a great start.

I made a mental note to find my bracelet after I ate. I was too hungry to look for it now. I reached around Gran and grabbed a plate. My stomach let out another loud grumble I felt to my core as I piled a little of everything onto my plate.

"Everything looks great," Gracie insisted as she reached for a plate.

"Thank you, dear," Gran said. "There's going to be a celebration dinner with the pack tonight. If either of you set out to do anything today, make sure you're back home before six."

"Okay," Gracie and I said in unison.

Having a celebratory potluck meal the night after a successful full moon run always happened. Everyone brought something to add to the mix. Generally, when someone was Moon Kissed, the dinner was more festive, though. It would most likely be extravagant this time because five of us had been Moon Kissed at once. It was a rare occurrence. In fact, I'd never seen it happen.

"I'm making my famous sugar rum cookies and bacon brussel sprouts," Gran said.

She never made her sugar rum cookies unless there was a special occasion to celebrate. I felt honored.

"I won't be late. We haven't had those in forever." My mouth watered at the thought of them.

"I can't wait!" Gracie insisted.

"Not only are we celebrating you and the others

becoming Moon Kissed, we're also celebrating the coming of a new birth to the pack."

"Really? Who's pregnant?" I asked around a fork full of pancake.

Gran's face dimmed. "Taryn."

My heart stalled out.

Glenn was still missing. He wasn't coming back on his own, and I didn't think Shane and his brothers were going to set him free anytime soon. Nothing was being done to find him. Everyone thought he'd finally had enough of Taryn and their constant fighting and hit the road.

"While the five of you becoming Moon Kissed is important, we also need to come together as a pack and support Taryn during her time of need," Gran said, pulling me from my thoughts.

I set my fork down. My ravenous appetite had vanished. "Has anyone said anything about Glenn? Is there any more news on him?" I knew there wouldn't be, but it seemed like the appropriate thing to ask.

Gran shook her head. "I'm afraid not."

"Do you think he left her?" Gracie asked. It broke my heart that she knew how real the possibility of someone leaving was firsthand.

"I'm don't know," Gran insisted.

"Why would he, though?" Gracie asked. She stabbed at her hash browns.

"Sometimes people do things we'll never be able to understand," Gran said as she prepared herself a plate.

A stillness settled over the three of us. I knew it was because we were all thinking of Mom.

Dad emerged from the back of the trailer. His limp was

back and his face was already etched in pain. Frustration rolled off him in waves. I wished I could help ease what he felt but knew I couldn't. No one could. Only pills and alcohol helped him anymore.

"Morning, girls," he said as he made his way into the kitchen with the use of his cane. He fixed himself a mug of coffee and reached for one of his pill bottles lining the counter. I watched as he dumped a couple pills into his hand and popped them in his mouth before taking a swig of coffee to wash them down. His gaze drifted to me as though he could feel my eyes on him. "Congratulations again, honey. I'm so happy for you."

"Thanks." I forced my eyes away from him. Seeing him in pain always killed me.

———

AFTER BREAKFAST, I dressed and found my bracelet. Once I had it secured on my wrist, I decided to go for a walk. I needed time to process what I'd learned about Taryn. Should I talk to Eli about it? Wasn't it time we told his dad what we knew about Glenn's disappearance? I wasn't sure what he'd do, but telling him seemed better than keeping the secret to ourselves any longer.

Especially now that there was a baby involved.

Dark clouds were rolling in when I stepped outside. The promise of rain lingered in the air, and I wondered if we'd have to postpone the celebration dinner tonight because of it. It wouldn't be the first. The last time it rained during a celebration dinner, the canopy a pack member had bought was destroyed by the downpour.

"Congratulations, Mina, dear," the Bell sisters said in unison as I passed their porch. I waved and flashed them a polite smile as I continued toward the woods. "Looks like rain. If you're heading to the lake for a swim, you best hurry."

"Yeah. I hope it holds off for the dinner tonight," I called back to them.

A gust of wind whipped through my hair. It was definitely going to storm tonight. I could smell the rain hanging in the air. A vehicle heading my way had me stepping off the gravel road so they could pass.

"Congratulations, Mina," another of the pack members said from inside the cab as it cruised by.

"Thank you," I called out to them before stepping back onto the road.

"In a hurry to get somewhere?" a familiar voice asked. The rich rumble of his voice had me pausing in my tracks as my stomach flip-flopped.

Eli sat on the wooden steps of his trailer. A burlap sack was on the ground between his legs, and there was a black trash bag to his left. He held an ear of corn, shucking it.

"No," I said even though I was positive he could tell it was a lie.

Of course I was in a hurry. My guilt from knowing what had happened to Glenn was suffocating me. I needed to submerge myself in nature so I could breathe.

"What is it, can't stand everyone congratulating you this morning?" he asked as he continued to peel back the silken husk of the golden corn. "Or is it that you heard about Taryn?"

"Both." I sighed as I tucked a stray hair behind my ear the breeze had released from my ponytail.

I moved to where he sat and grabbed an ear of corn from his bag, hoping chatting with him about it all would ease what I was feeling. My hands began the familiar process of prepping the corn to be eaten, and I felt my heart rhythm slow. The thoughts racing through my head chilled out, and I told myself it was from doing something I'd done a million times, not from being in Eli's presence. Gran purchased fresh corn from the farmer's market every summer. When she did, it was always mine and Gracie's job to shuck it for her. That was all this feeling was.

"I was shocked to hear about it, too," Eli insisted.

I chewed my bottom lip, unsure if I should voice the question pounding through my head.

"Do you think we should say something to your dad now?" The words propelled themselves past my lips on their own accord.

Eli shook his head. "I told you, he's busy with something else."

"This is important. This involves a member of our pack. It involves someone abducting members of our pack and selling them," I pressed. There was nothing more important than this. There couldn't be.

"Trust me. What my father is handling involves members of our pack as well. It's just as important, if not more so."

"I guess I just don't understand what could be more important than this."

Eli sighed. "I can't tell you, Mina. I would if I could, but I'm not at liberty to give you any details." A rawness entered his voice when he spoke. I believed him. If he could tell me, he would have. It must be big if he was sworn to silence. "Besides, we don't have any proof. We don't even know where Glenn was taken. What good would telling my dad what little we know do?"

"It would ease my conscience," I admitted. Eli didn't speak. Instead, he continued peeling off the corn husk and tossing it in the garbage bag beside him. "Don't you feel bad for keeping it to yourself?" I had to ask. How could I not? The guilt was what was eating at me most.

"Not particularly. It's not enough information for anyone to do anything with."

My stomach twisted. "Then we have to get more."

"I figured you'd come to that conclusion." He smirked as though he knew me so well. "How do you propose we do that?"

I thought for a second. "We can continue to scope out the woods at night and see if Shane or his brothers mention anything else about where Glenn was taken. We can check out his oldest brother's vet clinic, too. Maybe there's something there. A clue or something."

I tried to think of anything else we could do but came up short.

"Sounds like a plan."

I placed the ear of corn I'd shucked into a bucket on the step behind him and reached for another one. "Where did you get all this corn?"

"It was payment for a job I did. I helped one of the farmers in town mend their fence."

It didn't surprise me. Eli was always doing side jobs for trade. "What are you going to do with all of it? It's a lot of corn."

"Eat it," he said in a smart-ass tone.

I slapped him playfully on the shoulder. "Well, yeah. I figured that much."

"Seriously though, I'm using most of it tonight for the dinner. The rest I plan to blanch and freeze." He ripped off a handful of husk and shoved it in the black trash bag beside him. "You don't have to help. You can head to the lake, but before you go I have something for you."

He stood and reached into his pocket. My heart hammered against my rib cage. Eli had something for me?

When he pulled out a tiny silken sack and held it out to me, my curiosity piqued.

"You didn't have to get me anything," I said as it took the bag from him. It weighed almost nothing. My mind reeled with what might be inside.

"It's nothing major. Just something I thought you could use," he said as he repositioned himself on his step.

I loosened the drawstring top and dumped the tiny bag's contents into the palm of my hand. A silver ring spilled out. I plucked it from my palm and stared at a beautiful silver crescent moon attached to a silver band.

"You're going to have to wear silver more, you know. Gotta keep that wolf of yours in check. Plus, when I saw it in the shop, I thought of you," Eli said with a shrug of his shoulders.

"It's beautiful. Thank you," I said as I continued to stare at the ring. It was delicate and simple, but stunning. It was perfect.

"You're welcome. Put it on," Eli insisted. His eyes were on me. I could feel them. When I lifted my gaze to lock with his, I noticed how bright his eyes were. Emotions swirled through them that had my breath hitching in my throat and butterflies flapping. "See if it fits."

I slipped the ring onto the index finger of my right hand. "You got the right size."

"Good." Eli tossed another husk-free ear of corn into the basket behind him. He stood and reached for his front door. "You thirsty?"

I licked my lips. "Yeah, I could go for something. Got any soda?"

"No, but I've got apple pie moonshine." He winked.

"Is that all I'm ever going to drink over here?"

"Would that be a bad thing?"

"I guess it could always be worse." I laughed.

"So, is that yes?"

"Yeah, sure. I'll have a sip. After all, I am celebrating."

"Damn right you are. You're Moon Kissed now," Eli said before disappearing inside his trailer.

I grabbed another ear of corn and began shucking it. My cell chimed with a new text. It was Alec.

Hey, getting ready to head to Mirror Lake Diner for lunch. Want to come? I'm meeting Shane and Becca, plus Benji of course.

I reread his text, debating on how I could decline. It wasn't that I didn't want to hang out with him or some of his friends. Shane just ruined the scenario for me. Plus, I didn't want to dip out on Eli. A part of me wanted to hang around and help him shuck corn while I sipped apple pie moonshine.

Actually, I have to take my sister somewhere. Can I take a rain check? - Mina

Yeah, sure. No problem. Maybe we can hang

**out later this week, or even this weekend.
Definitely. - Mina**

I hated lying to him, but lunch might turn into dinner and I couldn't miss the celebration with my pack.

"Here you go," Eli said as he stepped out of his trailer. There was a red solo cup in both hands. "I poured it into a cup this time, since we're drinking outside. That way no one scolds me for allowing an underage girl to drink alcohol in my presence."

"Nice," I said as I shoved my cell back into my pocket. Eli handed me a cup, and I took it.

"Everything ok?" Eli asked as though he could pick up on the unease trickling through my system.

I tucked a few stray strands of hair behind my ear. "Yeah. Sure. Why wouldn't it be?"

"I don't know. You look like something is bothering you. Figured I'd ask."

Guilt trickled through me, but I was quick to force it away. There was no need to feel guilty. I was hanging out with my pack today, which included Eli. We were celebrating. All of us. Not just Eli and me.

"I'm fine," I said as I plastered a smile on.

"Yes, you are." Eli grinned. His eyes appraised my long legs and heat rushed to my cheeks. My grin grew until it crinkled the corners of my eyes, and I slapped him on the arm. "There's a real smile," he insisted. His eyes darkened with a heavy sense of determination I wasn't aware he possessed.

I licked my lips as the sticky heat of passion rushed across my skin from the look in his eyes. Eli leaned closer, his teeth skimming his bottom lip as his eyes remained locked on mine. He was going to kiss me. I should have moved, but I didn't. A part of me wanted his lips pressed against mine, to taste him across my tongue.

It was wrong, but it couldn't be denied.

Inches remained between us before I was able to get a damn grip. Everything about him had pulled me in, begging me to remain where I was, to let it happen.

I leaned away from him, but it was two seconds too late.

His lips brushed across mine, causing my entire body to respond at the feel of him. My stomach coiled as his tongue snaked out to tempt my mouth. I exhaled a tiny moan I was instantly ashamed of. Eli pulled away, sending shockwaves of heat pulsing through me. My body and mind went to war. One wanted more while the other could only think of Alec.

Sweet, southern, sexy Alec.

"I've always wanted to do that," Eli whispered, his breath caressing against my face.

My stomach somersaulted. Had I always wanted to kiss him too?

Eli placed distance between us, allowing me the space I needed to remember how to breathe. He lifted his cup in the air. "To being Moon Kissed." A wolfish grin spread across his face. "Finally."

"Yeah, finally," I said with a smile as I tapped my cup to his.

I took a swig of the liquid fire he'd poured for me and went back to shucking corn, trying to ignore the feeling his kiss had stirred to life inside me.

Celebrate.

That's what I was doing today. Everything else would come tomorrow.

THANK YOU

Thank you for reading *Moon Kissed*, I hope you enjoyed it! Please consider leaving an honest review at your point of purchase. Reviews help me in so many ways!

If you would like to know when my next novel is available, you can sign up for my newsletter here:
https://jennifersnyderbooks.com/want-the-latest/
Also, feel free to reach out and tell me your thoughts about the novel. I'd love to hear from you!
Email me at: jennifersnyder04@gmail.com

To see a complete up-to-date list of my novels, please take a moment to visit this page:
http://jennifersnyderbooks.com/book-list/

MINA'S STORY CONTINUES IN

MOON HUNTED
Mirror Lake Wolves - Book Two

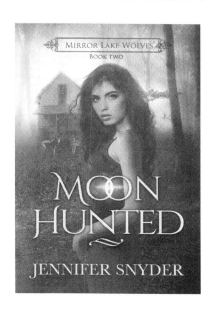

AVAILABLE NOW

Someone is hunting the Mirror Lake Wolves...

The woods of Mina's hometown are no longer safe. Glenn has been abducted and now so has another from the pack. Guilt eats at Mina because the one missing should have been her.

In fact, it was supposed to be.

Determined to find the young werewolf taken in her place, Mina and Eli go on a hunt. They hope to find Glenn along the way, but instead, discover the length they will go to ensure their own safety as well as the members of their pack.

Please Keep Reading for a Preview...

PREFACE

The air around me warmed; the old wolf magic came to the surface. It blew across my skin, ruffling my hair and sending it flying from my bun. A smile spread across my face as I lifted my arms high above my head. Strands of hair tickled my nose, but I ignored them. Instead, I waited for my wolf to come to me. When a chill slipped along my spine and goose bumps sprouted across my bare skin, I knew the goddess of the moon was near. Her magic danced through the air, calling to the wolf inside me. My wolf howled in response to her. It was a beautiful noise.

Lightness and loving warmth ignited my veins as the change intensified. The sensations spread throughout me until an overall sense of weightlessness became all I could feel.

I was air. I was light as a feather. I was free.

Pure love flooded my mind as the cold touch of the moon goddess disappeared from my spine to be replaced by an embrace from my wolf. Warmth and the sensation of being grounded and one with the earth trickled through my extremities.

We were one, my wolf and I.

ONE

I narrowed my eyes at the brown and black fluff ball Gracie held in her arms. He was cute, but I knew he would be a pain in my ass. I prayed Gran would tell Gracie she couldn't keep the puppy.

"Please. I promise I'll take care of him. You won't even know he's here," Gracie insisted.

The dullness of Gran's eyes brightened as she continued to stare at the little fellow. Shit. She was giving in.

"I'll do extra chores," Gracie promised as an added bonus. I knew she wouldn't follow through with them. She never did. Gran had to know this too.

"Where did you get him?" I asked, hoping to pause Gran's thought process. My hand fisted around the grocery list she'd given me earlier. "And who's paying for him? You don't have the money to buy a puppy."

The little guy was a Yorkie. I knew those puppies didn't run cheap. Not if they were a purebred with papers. There was no way my little sister could afford one on her own.

JENNIFER SNYDER

"It doesn't matter where he came from. What matters is that he needs a home," Gracie snapped at me before shifting her gaze back to Gran. "Can we keep him?"

Gran placed a hand on her hip. I tried to read her face, but her expression was unreadable. "He's going to be a lot of work."

"I can handle it," Gracie insisted.

This wasn't heading anywhere good. I needed to find a new angle.

"What about his food and shots? How are you going to come up with the money for those?" It was a logical question. One Gran couldn't ignore.

We weren't the wealthiest of people. In fact, money was always a sore subject in our house.

"He won't eat much. He's tiny. And I'll figure it out," Gracie grumbled, making it clear she didn't want me to be a part of the conversation.

Regardless of what she wanted, I had a right to insert myself. I lived here too.

"Mina does have a point. *If* I let you keep him, he'll be your responsibility. That means you're going to have to figure out how to come up with the money to get his shots and pay for his food," Gran said.

Great. It was a done deal.

I didn't hate dogs, or animals for that matter. I just didn't want my stuff peed on, pooped on, or chewed up. Wasn't that all puppies did the first year or three?

I smoothed a hand over my face and tried to contain myself. Why did my little sister always get what she wanted?

"I'll use the money I have saved from birthdays for his shots," Gracie insisted, clutching the puppy closer to her

226

chest. "His food won't be expensive, and I'm sure it'll last him a while. I can find ways to earn enough money to keep him fed."

"You'll have to because I won't buy food for him. I won't clean up after him either," Gran insisted. "I mean it when I say he's yours and yours alone."

It was a lie. I knew it the second the words came out of Gran's mouth. She'd buy food if he needed it because she wouldn't be able to watch him starve. She'd clean up after him from time to time, and she'd help take care of him. She'd expect me to do the same. While it might start off as though the fluff ball was Gracie's responsibility, there would come a point where he would become being everyone's. That was how it always was with any of Gracie's pets.

"So, I get to keep him?" Gracie's face lit up, making her look younger than her thirteen years.

The corners of my lips twitched upward at the sight of her smile. Seeing her happy was almost worth what I knew I was about to endure with the little beast. Almost.

"I don't see why not," Gran insisted, sealing the deal.

Happy squeals echoed through the living room of our trailer. Gracie jumped up and down, shaking the entire structure while clutching her new puppy to her chest. Once she calmed down, she kissed Gran on the cheek and headed to our shared room at the end of the hall, whispering to her new pet as she walked.

My lips pinched together as I fought to hold back the string of swear words building across my tongue. I'd cursed in front of Gran before, but she made it known it wasn't something she liked.

I couldn't keep my mouth shut though, no matter how hard I tried.

"I don't want that thing on my bed, Gracie! And he better not chew up any of my stuff!" I shouted after her. "Or shit in our room! I don't want to smell dog crap every time I walk in!"

Gran cleared her throat. My gaze drifted to her. I waited for her to scold me for cursing in her presence. "First of all, language. Second, have faith in her, Mina."

"Sorry. I'll try." I exhaled a long breath, then grabbed my wallet and keys from the kitchen counter. I relaxed my grip on the grocery list I held and took a step toward the front door. Never had I been so eager to head to the store. I needed to chill. I knew I did. Gracie getting a puppy wasn't the end of the world. I wasn't sure why it bothered me so much. "I'm heading out to get the stuff on your list."

"Ask Gracie if she wants you to pick up puppy food before you leave," Gran insisted.

I fought the desire to roll my eyes. Wasn't that something she was supposed to get all on her own? My blood simmered through my veins.

"He'll most likely get hungry once he settles down later, and I refuse to feed him scraps. It a horrible habit."

"Don't we have a bag somewhere from the last time she brought home a stray dog?"

Gracie was always bringing home animals, but puppies seemed to be her favorite. I'd lost count as to how many she'd brought home over the years.

"I gave it away," Gran said with a shake of her head. "Didn't think I'd agree to let her keep another one."

"I don't know why you did," I muttered as I started down the hall.

"I heard that," Gran snapped.

I didn't apologize.

Gracie was sprawled across her bed when I stepped into the room, the puppy tucked up against her side. He was curled into a ball, sleeping. It was cute but not cute enough.

All I could do was stare at its round belly and think about worms festering inside. Its furry ear twitched in its sleep and images of it being flea infested crept through my mind.

Gross.

"I'm leaving for the store. Gran gave me a list earlier," I said as I leaned against the doorframe. "Give me some money. I'll pick up a bag of dog food while I'm out."

Gracie slipped out of bed without speaking and stepped to her dresser. She swiped her piggy bank up and opened the bottom. The puppy wiggled around, adjusting itself into a tighter ball.

"Here." Gracie held out a twenty.

"Okay." I plucked it from her fingers and crammed it into my front pocket. "What kind of food should I get?"

"Any for small breed puppies, duh."

My teeth ground together as I stared at her. She was really pushing her luck with me today.

I pushed myself off the wall and started back down the hall.

"Be back in a bit," I called to Gran once I reached the front door.

Sticky heat rolled over me the instant I stepped foot outside, but anything was better than being indoors with my bratty little sister who always managed to get her way. I tugged my driver side door open and tossed my wallet and cell into the passenger seat before climbing in. The engine sputtered a few times before catching, but this was nothing new. My beater of a car had definitely seen better days. Either my dad needed to carve out some sober time to fix it during the next full moon, or he needed to fork over some of his beer money to pay for repairs. The money I made from babysitting Felicia's twins wasn't going to be enough.

I rolled my windows down all the way and backed out of our tiny gravel driveway. I headed toward the main entrance of Mirror Lake Trailer Park, but was forced to pause when a navy blue truck turned into the park. My heart skipped a beat; I knew who the owner of the truck was.

Eli lifted his fingers in a typical male wave as he crept to where I'd stopped. A wide smile graced his perfect lips, one that sent butterflies flapping through my stomach. When his truck window was flush with mine, he stopped. My stomach somersaulted as I waited for what he might say. We hadn't spoken much since he'd kissed me the other night. I'd done everything in my power to avoid him during the celebratory potluck meal and as much as I could since it without letting him handle things involving Glenn's disappearance on his own.

It wasn't easy.

Stupid universe. It never did let me stay away from him for long.

"Hey." The sound of his voice coerced all of my nerve endings to life in an instant. His arm muscles flexed and bulged as he moved to manually roll his window down farther. "Where you headed to?"

"Um...the grocery store," I said as my gaze drifted across

his broad shoulders, up his neck, and focused on his mouth that begged to be kissed. Everything I'd felt around Eli before becoming moon kissed, before he'd kissed me, had intensified tenfold in the last few days.

"Fun. Want to swing by my place when you get back?" he asked.

My mouth grew dry. "What for?"

If there was news on Glenn, I'd be more than happy to stop by but not for anything else. I couldn't. The things I felt for Eli were too hard to ignore now.

In fact, they scared me now more than they ever did.

A beautiful smile stretched across his face. "I bought a gallon of paint and would love help painting my bedroom."

His bedroom? That was one room I should never allow myself to be alone with him in. Sweet Jesus, my body began to overheat at the thought of what might happen.

"I can't." The words came out too fast and flustered. I cleared my throat. "I have plans with Alec tonight."

Eli's bright green eyes flashed at the mention of his name. Ever since we learned Alec's friend, Shane, and his older brothers were responsible for the disappearance of a pack member, Eli had been leerier than usual of me hanging around him. While I understood where he was coming from, Eli still needed to realize Alec wasn't Shane.

"Will Shane be there?" he asked. His voice had become rigid, and a vein was beginning to bulge along the side of his neck.

"I think so. It's supposed to be a double date. Well, more like a triple date really," I rambled even though I knew Eli couldn't care less how many people were joining Alec and me tonight. Still, I couldn't shut up. "Benji started dating someone. We're all supposed to hang out at Rosemary's Diner tonight." My lips clamped shut. I'd already given him too many details. Knowing Eli, he'd show up to make sure nothing happened to me. If he couldn't make it personally, he'd send one of his brothers. Especially if I slipped up and gave him the time we were meeting.

"Promise me you'll be careful." His eyes darkened as they locked with mine.

I licked my lips. "I'm always careful."

Tension rippled from him. He wasn't satisfied with my answer, but he also knew better than to push his luck.

"Right. Listen, if you get bored, or your night doesn't pan out the way you thought it would, you know you can always swing by my place and help paint." He winked. A tense smile twisted at the corners of his lips. He was trying to let go of whatever unease learning I'd be in Shane's presence tonight had caused him. "It's been a while since our last painting party."

Heat crept up my neck at the memory of Eli pressing against my backside while attaching his phone to the set of speakers plugged into the wall where I'd been painting.

It seemed like forever ago.

"I'll be sure to remember that," I said as I let my foot off the brake and inched my car forward. "And if I learn anything new tonight that might help find Glenn, I'll let you know."

"Good." The muscles in his jaw clenched tight. "Speaking of, we should set a time this week to discuss the next step in our plan to find him. Especially since scoping out that vet office the other night where his oldest brother works was such a bust."

I pressed my foot against the brake, coming to a stop again. "Yeah, wish we could have gotten inside to look around."

It had been stupid going to the place after it was closed anyway. I wasn't sure what we'd thought we'd find. All we'd done was make the animals go crazy.

"We need to find a way to get inside, one that doesn't come off as suspicious. I thought about getting a dog just to have a legitimate reason." Eli chuckled.

"You might not have to. Gracie brought home a puppy."

Eli arched a brow. He knew how many pets Gracie had brought home over the years. "And Gran let her keep it?"

"Yup." I didn't want to get into it. It would only irritate me again.

"Okay, well maybe this is a good thing. I mean, the timing couldn't be better."

My lips twisted into a frown. Although I hated to admit it, Gracie's puppy might be our saving grace.

"True. I could offer to drive Gracie and her puppy to the vet when the time comes for its next set of shots. I can sneak around while I'm there. See if anything catches my eye. We already know there aren't many employees. Shane's oldest brother, Peter, plus three staff members."

Eli shook his head. "No. I don't like the idea of you doing all the dirty work by yourself."

"Do you have a better idea? One that doesn't scream weirdo?" It would seem strange to both Gracie and Gran if Eli offered to take Gracie's puppy to the vet.

"And you offering to give Gracie a ride to the vet won't? Everyone knows how much you detest animals."

"I do not detest animals. I just don't like dogs. Or cats.

Or..." I was starting to see his point. "Okay, maybe I'm a fish person. Fish don't make a mess. They don't chew up shoes or claw you like a little monster from underneath the couch when you walk by."

The last cat Gracie brought home did that to me one too many times. It always managed to scare the shit out of me. I was glad she'd found a home for it with someone else at school.

"My point exactly. Your gran is going to know you're up to something if you volunteer."

Sylvie Hess pulled up behind Eli in her tan minivan. She smiled and waved, but I knew she wanted Eli and me to get out of her way. Something in her eyes said it all. A kid crying from somewhere inside her van found its way to my ears.

"Whatever. Let's talk about it later." I eased my foot off the brake again, allowing my car to roll forward. I didn't want to keep Sylvie waiting.

"Yeah. Don't forget, swing by my place and help paint if your night is too dull." Eli winked before gassing it.

While I waited for Sylvie to turn into the park, my mind raced with different scenarios of how I could offer to drive the little fur ball to his next vet appointment. It seemed like the only way we were getting inside the place. Well, short of breaking and entering. I wasn't sure we would find anything that might pertain to Glenn there, but a girl could hope.

TWO

By the time I made it to Rosemary's Diner, it was after five thirty. I scanned the place half expecting to find Lilly hanging all over Alec somewhere while she took his drink order, but she wasn't anywhere in sight. I tucked my long hair behind my ear and started toward where Alec sat at a table with his friends. My gaze drifted from one waitress to another as I walked. Lilly didn't seem to be working tonight, which was a relief. She wasn't someone I tolerated easily. It seemed like whenever I met Alec here and she was working, she blatantly flirted with him in front of me. While he didn't seem to pick up on it, I did and it pushed my damn buttons. Hard.

Some girls were real pieces of work.

"Hey." I waved as I neared their table, heading toward an open chair beside Alec. It was strange not sitting at the bar. Generally, that was where Alec could be found. At least the sweet tea in front of him was the same. "It's weird to see you eating at a table," I said to him as I sat.

"There weren't enough open stools at the bar," Becca answered for him. "This place is packed tonight."

"All the old people here for the summer from Florida," Benji said.

I glanced over my shoulder at the bar. Elderly people did occupy the majority of the stools. There was one seat open at the end of the bar. Definitely not enough for the six of us.

Speaking of six...

We were missing someone, and it wasn't Shane.

"I thought you were bringing a date tonight, Benji," I said with a smile. Out of Alec's guy friends, he was my favorite. Benji was funny, sweet, and way more accepting of me than Shane—for obvious reasons. "What happened?"

"She'll be here," Benji said as he took a sip from his sweet tea.

He seemed nervous, which I found adorable. Add that to the collared shirt he wore, which I figured was probably from the church clothes section of his closet, and I wanted to reach across the table and pinch his chubby cheeks. Generally, Benji was a dirty blue jeans and plain cotton tee type of guy. I imagined when he stood up his jeans would be free of dirt, and he'd have on his good pair of boots. Not the ones always caked in mud.

"We haven't decided if Benji's girl is imaginary or real yet," Shane teased. His eyes didn't shift to me, even though his words seemed directed my way when he spoke. Ever since I'd become moon kissed, his intolerance of me had intensified.

Could he feel the change in me since the last full moon?

"Don't give me that crap," Benji grumbled. "You know

she's real. Hell, y'all probably had a class or two with her this past year."

I wondered who she was. Why hadn't I thought to ask Alec what her name was when he mentioned a triple date with her and Benji? At the thought of him, Alec's hand found my thigh beneath the table. He gave it a gentle squeeze, gaining my attention. I leaned toward him and pecked his cheek in a featherlight kiss. It was a simple gesture, but I didn't miss the smirk cutting across his face from it.

"Hey," he said. His deep brown eyes lit up as he flashed me a beautiful smile.

It had been too long since we'd hung out. I knew it was my fault. I'd blown him off so many times the last few days for pack related things, and now that I was in his presence, I regretted having done so. Alec was a great guy.

I returned his smile with one of my own. "Hey, yourself."

"I ordered you a water with lemon." His thumb made small circles along the smooth skin of my thigh. Tiny pulses of electricity jolted through my core at the feel of his touch.

"Thanks." I reached for the glass. My eyes drifted to Shane for whatever reason. He stared at my hand, zeroing in on something that seemed to surprise him. I knew what he saw.

The ring Eli had given me.

The silver ring with a tiny crescent moon soldered to the band. Part of me thought I should hide it, but a larger part argued there was no point. He'd already seen it. It was too late now.

Shane's gaze traveled to the bracelet my dad and Gran had given me next. My heart beat triple time as his gaze turned cold. If that wasn't enough proof to confirm whatever theories he might have had about me, I wasn't sure what more he'd need.

The tiny hairs on the back of my neck stood on end as Shane's gaze lifted to lock with mine.

"Interesting jewelry you have there," he said.

I kept my gaze on him, refusing to look away. Now was definitely not the time to show signs of unease. I needed to appear strong. Sure of myself. Lethal if screwed with. "Thanks. They were both gifts."

"Oh, really?" Shane's head tipped to the side as a wry smirk stretched across his face. Alec and Benji started talking about something besides me, but I tuned them out anticipating what question would spur from Shane's lips next. "What for?"

And there it was. Shane arched a brow as though challenging me to speak the truth about my silver jewelry.

How much did he know about my kind? Obviously, his knowledge was more than I felt comfortable with. There weren't many who knew werewolves existed, let alone of our need to wear silver.

"Beautiful. I really like the ring," Becca blurted out. I could have kissed her I was so damn happy for the interruption.

"Thanks," I said as I averted my eyes from Shane to lock with hers.

"I've always had a fascination with the moon." Becca grinned. "It's so beautiful and mysterious."

I opened my mouth to agree with her, but noticed a girl with dark curls bouncing around her shoulders walking toward us. She pushed her glasses up on her nose when she noticed me watching her, and her cheeks tinted pink as though she was embarrassed.

"She's here," Benji muttered as he straightened his back and eyed her. Immediately, he became hypnotized by the sight of her.

"Hi, everyone. Sorry I'm late. I had to help my aunt with something." The girl's blue eyes shifted around the table as her thin lips twisted into a friendly smile.

I remembered seeing her around school. She was new.

"You're good. We haven't ordered yet. Mina just got here, too." Benji pointed to me.

Her shoulders relaxed. "Cool."

Benji stood and pulled the chair beside him out for her. "Guys, this is Ridley. You probably remember her from school. She moved here from Pennsylvania a few months back."

"I remember seeing you around," I said while trying to think of what else I knew about her.

"Me too," Alec insisted. "You're related to the Caraways, right? The ones who own the inn."

"Yeah. That's my aunt," Ridley said as she situated herself in the chair beside Benji.

My guard went up at the mention of the Caraway family. While I didn't know them on a personal level, I knew they weren't typical residents of Mirror Lake.

The women were witches.

Gran had told me once they descended from a strong line of old magic. Their magic helped my pack keep our full moon rituals hidden from prying eyes. In return, we made sure vampires who weren't part of the Montevallo family, stayed out of Mirror Lake.

"People say that inn is haunted," Shane said. I shouldn't have been surprised by his bold words or the level of suspicion ringing through them, but I was.

Something about Shane always had him reverting to the supernatural.

"People say a lot of things," Benji grumbled, making it clear he didn't like where the conversation was headed.

"True." Shane shifted his attention to me, spearing me with a pointed gaze. "Doesn't mean they're wrong, though."

A chill swept up my spine, but I still managed to keep my eyes glued to his.

"How are you liking Mirror Lake so far? Has the heat gotten to you yet?" Becca asked. Again, she'd cut the tension when it was about to come to a head. "I'm sure your summers were mild in Pennsylvania, at least compared to this."

"You have no idea." Ridley laughed. "We had hot summers in Pennsylvania, but it was nothing compared to this. I'm surprised I haven't melted yet."

"You'll get used to it," Becca insisted before taking a sip from her water. "Did you live in a big city there?"

"Sort of. It was a little bigger than this, but not by much."

"What made you move to Mirror Lake?" Shane asked. His eyes were glued to her in the same cautious and skeptical way he always looked at me.

Ridley blinked, and the smile on her face disappeared, giving the impression that whatever reason she had for moving here wasn't one she cared to talk about.

"Um...family stuff." She tucked a few curls behind her ear and met Shane's gaze.

Our waitress came to ask Ridley what she wanted to drink and see if we were ready to place an order. Benji insisted on getting an order of fried pickles. He said it was a Rosemary's Diner must. We placed an order for some and asked for a few more minutes to glance over the menu. I didn't need any more time, though. I knew what I wanted. My usual—a cheeseburger and fries. I set my menu on top of Alec's and glanced at Ridley.

What type of magic did she have?

I studied her while she glanced over the menu. No inkling of the magic inside her called to me. Although maybe that wasn't something I could do. One would think becoming moon kissed would allow me to feel things—if other supernaturals were nearby and what magic they harbored, if any. I got nothing, though. Especially when I looked at her.

Maybe Ridley Caraway had no magic.

AVAILABLE NOW

ABOUT THE AUTHOR

Author
Jennifer Snyder

Jennifer Snyder lives in North Carolina where she spends most of her time writing New Adult and Young Adult Fiction, reading, and struggling to stay on top of housework. She is a tea lover with an obsession for Post-it notes and smooth writing pens. Jennifer lives with her husband and two children, who endure listening to songs that spur inspiration on repeat and tolerate her love for all paranormal, teenage-targeted TV shows.

To get an email whenever Jennifer releases a new title, sign up for her newsletter at https://jennifersnyderbooks.com/want-the-latest/. It's full of fun and freebies sent right to your inbox!

Find Jennifer Online!
jennifersnyderbooks.com/
jennifersnyder04@gmail.com

47104564R00148